Nicki Bennett

THE CATTLE BARON'S BOGUS BOYFRIEND

REAMSPUN DESIRES

PUBLISHED BY
REAMSPINNER
PRESS

Published by
DREAMSPINNER PRESS

5032 Capital Circle SW, Suite 2, PMB# 279,
Tallahassee, FL 32305-7886 USA
www.dreamspinnerpress.com

The Cattle Baron's Bogus Boyfriend © 2016 Nicki Bennett.

Cover Design © 2016 Bree Archer
http://www.breearcher.com
Cover content is for illustrative purposes only and any person depicted
on the cover is a model.

ISBN: 978-1-63477-018-7
Digital ISBN: 978-1-63477-019-4
Library of Congress Control Number: 2016904919
Published May 2016
v. 1.0

Printed in the United States of America

"I wasn't sure you were planning to attend," Eloise said with a hint of accusation.

Her gaze flickered over Jonah like a splash of ice water. "You remember your father's friend Franklin Meredith?" Linc nodded to her escort. "Franklin, my stepson Lincoln and his… guest… Jonah Hollis."

Jonah shook Franklin's hand. "Pleased to meet you, sir."

"I was just speaking with Melissa," Eloise observed as if Jonah hadn't spoken. "She's looking lovely, as always. Much too sweet for that crude John Maxwell." Jonah followed her glance to where Melissa stood in the next room, her blonde hair loose around the shoulders of a clinging black dress with a deep vee neckline filled with sheer gauze. When she rather pointedly turned her back to them, Jonah could see it was cut just as deeply there too.

"I suppose it was kind of you to invite your assistant to accompany you," Eloise continued. "I'm certain an opportunity like this hasn't come his way before."

Which Jonah supposed was a polite way of saying she thought he had no business being there, but Linc put an arm around Jonah's waist and met Eloise glare for glare.

"Jonah isn't here as my assistant," he said. "He's my date."

WELCOME TO

DREAMSPUN DESIRES

Dear Reader,

Love is the dream. It dazzles us, makes us stronger, and brings us to our knees. Dreamspun Desires tell stories of love featuring your favorite heartwarming heroes, captivating plots, and exotic locations. Stories that make your breath catch and your imagination soar.

In the pages of these wonderful love stories, readers can escape to a world where love conquers all, the tenderness of a first kiss sweeps you away, and your heart pounds at the sight of the one you love.

When you put it all together, you find romance in its truest form.

Love always finds a way.

Elizabeth North

Executive Director
Dreamspinner Press

Growing up in Chicago, **NICKI BENNETT** spent every Saturday at the central library, losing herself in the world of books. A voracious reader, she eventually found it difficult to find enough of the kind of stories she liked to read and decided to start writing them herself.

To the group at 44 1/2 (you know who you are) who talked me into writing this in the first place; to Ariel for constant encouragement along the way; and to Damon for helping craft the perfect title.

Chapter One

"I DON'T care if he's busy! I want to speak to him right now!"

Jonah Hollis bit back a sigh. "I'm sorry, Ms. Cutler, but I can't disturb Mr. Courtwright when he's in a meeting." *And you should know that by now*, he added silently. *You've been dating him for over six months.*

"If he knew this was the fifth time I called, he'd want you to let me talk to him now!"

It was actually the sixth time, but Jonah knew better than to correct her. He also knew better than to interrupt his boss during a meeting, no matter how far past the scheduled time it lasted. Lincoln Courtwright owned the Broken Spoke ranch—and the oil and natural gas reserves beneath it—and Jonah might only have been his administrative assistant a little longer than Melissa

Cutler had been dating him, but he knew how much Mr. Courtwright hated disruptions, especially when he was negotiating a new gas lease. Jonah wasn't about to risk his job for anything, especially not his boss's shrewish girlfriend. *She can't possibly talk to him this way, or he'd never stay with her. I guess a mere admin doesn't rate the same courtesy as a millionaire.* "I can assure you I'll give him your messages as soon as his meeting is over," he said in what he hoped was a soothing voice.

Apparently it wasn't soothing enough. "Maybe I haven't made myself clear. I need to talk to him *now*!"

Jonah wished he had an old-fashioned handset like the one on his parents' phone back on the farm, rather than the wireless headset he wore, so he could hold it away from his ear while Melissa continued her rant. She did have some reason to be upset, he admitted in an effort to remain calm. Mr. Courtwright's meeting with the prospective new gas drillers was already ninety minutes over schedule. *It's a good thing I don't have class tonight*, he thought when he checked the clock on his computer terminal. *Already past six thirty. I'd never make it in time. I hope that means the negotiations are going well.*

When Melissa finally seemed to be winding down, he interjected, "I don't imagine it will be too much longer, Ms. Cutler. I promise I'll let him know how urgent it is for him to call you as soon as he's free."

"Don't bother," she replied scornfully. "I had reservations for seven o'clock at Five Sixty to celebrate my win at the Tunica rodeo, but he'll never be ready in time, and I need to leave tonight for Tulsa." Melissa was an up-and-coming barrel racer on the Women's Professional Rodeo Association circuit, and Jonah knew from experience it could be challenging to coordinate their schedules, between her travel and his boss splitting time between the Dallas office and the ranch. Thanks to his roommate Wes, a devoted foodie, Jonah knew that Five Sixty was the new restaurant Wolfgang Puck had opened at the top of Reunion Tower, offering Asian fusion cuisine with a rotating view of the Dallas skyline from 560 feet in the air. It was also one of the most expensive restaurants in the city.

"I know he'll be sorry to have missed it," he said with genuine concern.

"He won't know what he's missing if he isn't careful," she snapped before ending the call.

Jonah pulled the headset off his ear and arched to stretch his back. He'd finished his work for the day at least an hour ago, but he didn't like to leave the office while Mr. Courtwright was still in a meeting, in case he needed something done when it was over. He was straightening his desk when the door to the inner office finally opened and his boss came out, escorting two distinctly unhappy-looking men in suits.

For just a moment, Jonah let himself appreciate the contrast between the two buttoned-down corporate reps and his boss's casual style. Mr. Courtwright wore jeans and a simple white dress shirt, sleeves rolled up to bare his muscled forearms, sprinkled with the same tawny, slightly shaggy hair that brushed his collar. *Need to schedule him an appointment for a haircut*, Jonah thought as Mr. Courtwright escorted the men to the door.

"Are you sure you won't reconsider?" one of them asked.

"What part of 'hell no' don't you understand?" Mr. Courtwright all but growled. "I won't have fracking on my land. I don't care if it means never pumping another cubic foot of gas out of the ground. Now get out of here, and tell your boss not to bother contacting me again." Jonah had the feeling he would have slammed the office's thick glass outer door behind them if he could.

When they were out in the hall and headed toward the elevators, Mr. Courtwright turned, running his hands through his hair, and seemed startled to notice Jonah at his desk. "Why are you still here, Jonah? I didn't mean for you to wait for me to wrap it up with those idiots."

And that was why Jonah was halfway in love with Lincoln Courtwright. Not only was the man as handsome as sin, with a lean, muscled body that showed he still took an active part in the day-to-day workings of his cattle ranch, but he genuinely cared about his employees. "Ms. Cutler called several times for you, and I promised I'd get you the messages."

"Oh hell, I forgot she wanted to have dinner tonight. Did she say where?"

"She mentioned a reservation at Five Sixty, but it was for seven o'clock."

Jonah checked the time on his computer while Mr. Courtwright glanced at his watch and groaned. "I guess I'm in the doghouse again. Though if I wanted to spin around while I'm eating, I'd get a corny dog and ride the Ferris wheel at the state fair." Jonah bit back an unprofessional giggle. "I guess I better call her and apologize."

"She said she had to leave tonight for the rodeo in Tulsa tomorrow," Jonah added.

"I'm screwed, aren't I?" Mr. Courtwright ran a hand through his hair again. "Send her a dozen roses— better make it two dozen. And pick her out one of those tennis bracelets she likes. She really loved the one you got for her birthday."

"Yes, sir," Jonah said. The company credit card he used for office purchases was going to get a workout, but he couldn't really begrudge Melissa her apology.

"What have I told you about calling me sir? This isn't the Army."

"Yes, Mr. Courtwright," Jonah corrected himself.

His boss frowned. He'd asked Jonah several times to call him Linc, but Jonah couldn't bring himself to be that familiar—not when it might give away how much more familiar he wished he could be.

"I'm looking forward to a long weekend at the ranch," Mr. Courtwright continued. "If I can't punch idiots like those two, I might as well punch cattle instead." He shook his head. "After the recent studies showing the link between fracking and the increase in earthquakes in the Dallas area, they still tried to convince me it was all a coincidence. And that I shouldn't care anyway, since it would mean more profits for me. And for them, of course." He shared a rueful smile with Jonah. "Don't take any more calls from them, and take a look into the other firms that have sent in proposals. See who else they have leases with and what kind of methods they use. I don't want to waste any more time with companies that think fracking is the only way to go."

Jonah jotted a note on his pad.

"And see if you can find another source for organic hay. The cattle are fine with grass for now, especially with all the rain we had this spring, but it meant a delay in sowing the feed crops, and our regular supplier may not be able to meet all our needs for the winter. I'd rather find another source now than have to scramble come fall and probably pay more because everyone else is doing the same thing."

Jonah made another note. Since Linc had taken over the Broken Spoke at his father's death, he'd turned the cattle operation to natural, grass-fed, chemical-free methods that cost more than traditional ranching but allowed him to charge premium rates for organic beef. The last time he'd gone home to Oktaha, Jonah had suggested to his father that he consider switching to organic methods on the farm, where he grew hay for the local cattle ranches. There was growing demand for organic feed, but his father was slow to change, and since his relationship with his parents had been strained ever since Jonah had come out to them—and the rest of his hometown—as gay, he hadn't pushed the idea.

"I'll take care of it," Jonah assured him, turning toward his computer.

"I didn't mean this minute! It can wait until tomorrow. C'mon, I'll walk out with you."

As much as he was tempted, Jonah shook his head. "Thanks, but I want to take care of Melissa tonight." Just because he had a hopeless crush on his boss didn't mean he would do anything to jeopardize Linc's relationship with his girlfriend. "Besides, I promised my roommate I'd meet him for a late dinner after he gets off work, so I'm in no rush." That was a bit of a white lie—Wes worked as a waiter/bartender at Prism, a restaurant not far from where they lived, and had issued Jonah a standing invitation to come in for dinner any night he could, but Jonah didn't feel right about taking advantage of his friend's generosity when he owed him so much already. Still, it would work as an excuse for not leaving with Linc.

"You take such good care of me." Linc smiled, and Jonah melted a little inside. He'd do anything in his power to earn more of those smiles. "Don't stay too late."

"I won't, Mr. Courtwright. Have a safe drive back to the ranch. Don't let that truck of yours break down on the way."

That won Jonah a full-out laugh. Jonah had been shocked to learn that his boss, who could afford any luxury car made, preferred to drive around in a beat-up Ford F-150 pickup. Jonah drove a similar truck himself—it was the farm workhorse until his father had replaced it with a newer model back when Jonah graduated from high school—but Linc's had even more miles on it. "I will. You drive safe too."

Jonah's commute was much shorter; it never took him more than twenty minutes to get from downtown to the townhouse he and Wes shared with two other friends in the eclectic Bishop Arts District, while the Broken Spoke was a good two hours or more west of Dallas. Linc had a condo in the Design District he used on the nights he stayed in the city for business, but he spent as much time as he could working on the ranch.

"I will, thanks. Night, Mr. Courtwright."

"Night, Jonah."

Once his boss left, Jonah turned his attention to his computer screen. Ordering two dozen roses was easy. He googled the rodeo website and found the host hotel, then made a quick phone call to confirm Melissa was registered. He arranged to have the roses delivered there so she wouldn't have to wait until she returned home on Monday to see the apology he dictated in Linc's name. Selecting a bracelet took a bit longer. Melissa was tall and slender, with long blonde hair and blue eyes. It was easy to understand what Linc saw in her, and when she wasn't shouting at him over the phone, Jonah had to admit she seemed to be nice enough. She just didn't make allowances for the time it took Linc to run two businesses and do both well, with concern for the environment as well as for the profit they could bring.

Jonah's stomach growled, dragging his attention away from his boss's attributes and back to the matter at hand. After finally selecting a slender bracelet set with sapphires that cost more than his monthly rent, he placed the order to be delivered to Melissa's home address and then shut down his computer for the night. He set the lock on the office door and headed toward the parking garage for his truck. Maybe he'd stop and get something to eat at Prism after all. He'd just have to convince Wes to let him pay.

Chapter Two

JONAH had to circle the block twice to find a parking space within walking distance of Prism. The restaurant had turned its small parking slab into a patio, and even in the heat of a late-August evening in Dallas, the picnic tables, covered by a canvas awning outlined with twinkling lights and cooled by misters, were filled with people. Jonah considered that a good sign, given what Wes had told him about how many small restaurants failed within their first six months. Prism was going on a year now and seemed to have found a niche with its eclectic menu based on locally sourced, seasonal ingredients.

The hostess nodded at him when he entered and pointed toward the bar, where he could see Wes behind the counter made from a pair of old wooden doors. He weaved his way between tables and took a vacant stool, waiting until Wes finished with the customer he was serving before waving to announce his presence.

"Are you just getting off work?" Wes asked. The bar was small enough that he could mix the drink order and still talk with Jonah. "What did that slave driver of a boss of yours have you doing this late?"

"Mr. Courtwright isn't a slave driver!" Jonah was quick to protest. "He didn't ask me to work late, and when he got out of his meeting, he told me I shouldn't have stayed." It's not like he had anything more important to do, Jonah thought, except for the two nights a week he attended the business class he was taking at El Centro community college.

Wes walked the drink he'd been making to the other end of the bar and started mixing another before answering. "So why did you stay, then? I know you've got the hots for him, but if he was in a meeting, you didn't even get to spend the time with him."

Jonah flushed, but before he could issue a denial, Wes wagged a finger at him.

"And don't try to tell me you don't have the hots for him. I've spent too many nights listening to 'Mr. Courtwright said this' and 'Mr. Courtwright did that.' I like the guy I work for too, but I don't talk about him constantly."

"It doesn't matter how hot he is," Jonah muttered. "He's straight. I stayed late to order gifts for his girlfriend to make up for him missing dinner with her because *he* was working late."

"You need to forget about him and come out with Aidan and Sammy and me tomorrow night instead," Wes declared, setting the drink he'd been mixing in front of Jonah. "Try that and tell me what you think."

"You know I'm not much of a drinker," Jonah said. "I don't really like the taste of alcohol."

"That's why you're the perfect taste-tester," Wes replied. "If you like it, I know I've got a winner."

Jonah picked up the glass of icy liquid and sniffed it. He could smell citrus and a hint of something else, though he couldn't tell what it was. "What's in it?"

"I've been experimenting with making some vodka infusions. That one's basil with lime juice and a bit of grapefruit juice, topped off with sparkling water. What do you think?"

Jonah took a small sip and then a larger one. "I like it. It's tart and refreshing, especially on a hot night like this."

"Great! If Mr. Stefanotis likes it, maybe he'll put it on the menu." Wes grinned. "It's not working in the kitchen, but it's a start."

Jonah grinned back. Wes Paterson didn't look like anyone's idea of a traditional chef. His spiked hair was currently dyed a deep blue, though he changed its color every month or so—Jonah didn't think he'd seen its natural color in the year and a half they'd lived together. He was wearing a colorful flowered shirt that didn't hide the tattoos on his arms, and both ears and an eyebrow sported piercings. Despite his appearance, he was the best cook Jonah knew, even better than his mother, which was saying something. He was also the kindest person Jonah knew, except maybe for his best friend, Caylee, back in Oktaha. Not many people would take a total stranger under his wing the way Wes had when Jonah first arrived in Dallas.

"So what's good for dinner tonight?" Jonah asked, turning to look toward the front door at the blackboard that was the restaurant's only menu. While a few offerings, like the three-pepper mac and cheese and the fried chicken, were mainstays, the rest of the menu depended on what produce was fresh and what Manny, the head cook, felt like making that day.

"Aidan raved about the brisket tacos, and Sammy had the mushroom quinoa risotto." Aidan Jacobs and Samuel Tanner lived in the townhouse that made up the other half of the building he and Wes shared, though the four of them were in and out of each other's space so much they might as well have all been living together.

"Are they here? I didn't see them at a table when I came in."

"They went to do some shopping, but they said they'd be back before closing time."

Jonah decided on the fried green tomato BLT on whole-grain toast from Lembas Bakery, a local shop owned by a lesbian couple who made amazing breads and pastries. He was just finishing up the last of the homemade potato chips that came with the sandwich when Aidan and Sammy arrived, carrying bags from Urban Vintage, a clothing store down the street.

"Jonah!" Sammy said loudly. "Tell me you did not come here straight from work. You're giving gay men a bad name, dressed like that."

"What's wrong with the way I'm dressed?" Jonah asked. He didn't think his khakis and pale blue dress shirt looked bad, though maybe they'd gotten a little wrinkled between the long day and the heat.

"Have we taught you nothing, child?" Sammy waved a hand to indicate his and Aidan's attire. Jonah thought the rich purple V-neck Sammy wore contrasted beautifully with his dark skin, while Aidan's green-and-white paisley accented his pale complexion and red hair, even though neither of them were shirts he'd be comfortable wearing. "It's too late to take you shopping now, but I'm coming to look through your closet before we go clubbing tomorrow night. If we can't find anything fit to be seen with you in, you can borrow something from one of us."

"I wouldn't fit in anything of yours," Jonah pointed out. He certainly wasn't heavy, but Sammy was half a head taller and at least twenty pounds lighter than he was, while Aidan was built like the construction worker he was.

"Sure you would," Aidan said. "They just wouldn't hang on you the way most of your shirts do. You've got a good build. You ought to show it off."

Tight-fitting shirts weren't very practical for working on a farm, but if Jonah said that, he knew they'd just remind him he didn't live on a farm anymore. And he didn't have to dress to hide the fact that he was gay anymore either. But that didn't make him any more eager to wear clinging shirts and skintight jeans to attract attention in the clubs Sammy and Aidan wanted to take him to. "Maybe I'll just skip tomorrow night."

"Absolutely not!" Wes interjected. "You deserve a night out after working late today. And besides, the best way to get over your crush on your boss—your straight boss, as you pointed out to me yourself—is to find someone who is interested in you."

He'd never say it to Wes, but sometimes Jonah wondered whether his three friends thought he didn't measure up as a gay man. He was far more comfortable in his work clothes or the jeans and chambray shirts he wore back home than the bright colors they wanted to dress him in. And he'd rather stay home with a good book, or even his economics homework, than spend a night making the club scene. Sammy and Aidan were a committed couple, so while they loved dancing, it was only with each other or with friends who knew they were together. Wes was a party animal, socializing with everyone, even if he was very selective about who he spent time with as more than a casual acquaintance. When they'd first met, Jonah had thought maybe Wes was trying to pick him up, but Wes made it clear he was only looking for a roommate to help share expenses, not a bed partner. And while Jonah had met plenty of attractive men since coming to Dallas, he hadn't felt a spark of attraction for any of them.

Until the day he'd gone to work for Lincoln Courtwright.

Linc was everything that appealed to Jonah in a man: handsome without being vain; intelligent without being condescending; self-assured without being arrogant. He could dress to the nines and appreciate culture, as Jonah had seen on the night Linc had taken Melissa to the Texas Ballet Theater. But then he'd come into the office in jeans and run-down boots and confessed to Jonah that he couldn't wait to get back to the ranch and work with the new horse he'd bought. Jonah had been attracted to him from the start, when he was just on a temp assignment to update the Broken Spoke's cattle records. He hadn't had much contact with the boss then—he worked most closely with Linc's administrative assistant at the time, Jennifer Wagner— though Linc always greeted him and stopped to say a few words whenever he walked through the office when Jonah was working. Jennifer must have been impressed with Jonah's efforts, because when she decided to be a stay-at-home mom after becoming pregnant with her second child, she recommended Jonah take her place. Since then, working closely with Linc every day he was in the office had only strengthened Jonah's attraction. He was afraid no other man would measure up.

Which was a problem, since Linc was straight. And even if he weren't, Jonah knew he didn't have anything to attract a man like Lincoln Courtwright. He was an Oklahoma farm boy with a few years of community college under his belt. He had a decent build, though it had softened a bit now that he wasn't helping on the farm or loading trucks at the transportation company he'd worked at to pay for his college classes before leaving Oktaha. He had short brown hair and unremarkable features and nothing at all to appeal to a rich and handsome man like his boss.

Maybe Wes is right, Jonah thought. *I'm never going to get over this hopeless crush if I don't try to meet someone else.* But that was part of the problem. Most of the guys he met in the clubs Wes and Aidan and Sammy dragged him to were looking for a good time, not a commitment. Jonah had nothing against having a good time, but he wasn't interested in just being some stranger's one-night stand. He had the example of his own parents, who had married out of high school and still seemed as much in love as ever, and his father's parents, who had been married for seventy-one years. His grandmother had passed away within weeks of his grandfather, as if she couldn't bear to live without him. He wanted that kind of relationship, but he supposed he'd have to make the effort to meet someone first.

"Okay," he said, "I'll go with you tomorrow night. But I'm picking my own clothes!"

Chapter Three

THE next day at work seemed to drag, though Jonah recognized that was as much because Linc wasn't in the office as because it was Friday. Linc tried to spend two or three days a week in Dallas, dealing with the paperwork, phone calls, and meetings required to keep both the cattle business and the oil and gas leases running smoothly. That he didn't have to spend every day in the city was due in part to Jonah's efforts in screening phone calls and e-mails and written correspondence. He dealt with the routine matters himself and did background prep on the more involved ones, pulling past files or summarizing information to make it easier for Linc to take the appropriate action and make the tough decisions.

Jonah knew a little about cattle ranching from the relationships his father had forged with the local grazing outfits that bought their hay, but the small ranches and family farms he was accustomed to weren't a patch on the Broken Spoke. The land had been in the Courtwright family since just after the Civil War, and while it wasn't anywhere near the biggest ranch in Texas, it ran thousands of head of cattle and spread across parts of three counties. Linc made no secret of the fact that he'd just as soon spend all his time on the ranch if he could, but he was too shrewd a businessman, and too good a steward of the family resources, to ignore the energy reserves that now made up the bigger part of his income.

Jonah knew next to nothing about oil and gas production, though since becoming Linc's administrative assistant he'd done some reading, and he found it fascinating. Linc felt as strongly about environmental conservation as he did about organic ranching, which could be challenging in an industry that valued production and profit above all else. After researching the proposals that had been submitted to replace the current company managing the drilling on the Broken Spoke, Jonah found none of them any better than the group Linc had kicked out of the office the day before when it came to environmentally safe, low-impact methods. Making a note to do more research into other producers, Jonah set the proposals aside and focused on finding additional sources of organic feed instead. He was much more successful there, and identified three different providers and requested quotes from each. He'd be able to offer Linc several options by the time he returned to the office next week.

Deciding he'd accomplished everything he could for the day, Jonah shut down his computer and closed up the office. Even though it was barely four o'clock, traffic leaving downtown was heavy, the seemingly eternal construction on the three major interstates that passed through the central business district adding to the backups. Jonah avoided the highways and took surface streets, crossing the arching new Calatrava bridge over the Trinity River before passing through Oak Cliff to the townhouse he and Wes shared in the Bishop Arts District.

Wes's scooter was already in the backyard when Jonah parked his truck along the curb on the side of the two-story brick building. The house was split vertically into two units, each with a kitchen and open living room/dining area on the first floor and two bedrooms on the second, though Sammy had turned one of the bedrooms on their side into a home office for his graphic design business.

"Honey, I'm home," Jonah called as he dropped his backpack into the cubby beside the front door. He didn't see Wes, but a delicious aroma filled the open space. "What smells so good?"

"I've got enchiladas verdes in the oven," Wes answered as he came down the stairs. "The shower's free if you want to clean up and change before we eat."

"I'd better wait. With my luck I'd get sauce on my shirt, and I'm not changing more than once." He glanced at the blue-and-orange patterned crew neck Wes wore over a pair of Lucky jeans. When Wes bent down to check the casserole in the oven, the top crept up to reveal a few inches of smooth skin.

"Well, you'd better decide what you plan to wear before Sammy and Aidan get here, or Sammy will be pawing through everything in your closet to find something 'appropriate.'"

As if summoned by Wes's comment, Aidan and Sammy walked in through the back door, carrying a bowl of guacamole and a bag of chips. "We could smell the Mexican next door, so Sammy whipped up a batch of guac."

"Enchiladas will be ready in just a few minutes. Grab a beer from the fridge if you want."

Aidan was already pulling a bowl for the chips out of a cabinet when Sammy stopped in front of Jonah. "You are planning on changing, yes?"

"Yes, though I'm not letting you anywhere near my closet," Jonah said with a smile. Sammy was wearing a pair of bright yellow slacks that clung to his long legs and a turquoise jacket with the sleeves rolled up. Aidan had on cuffed jeans and a dark red tank top that molded to his chest and showed off muscular arms from his work in construction.

"Eat first, criticize Jonah's lack of fashion sense later," Wes insisted, setting a bubbling casserole dish on a hot pad in the center of the table. He pulled out a second tray and set it beside the first. "This one's chicken, and Sammy, this one's rajas y queso for you. Help yourself to plates and silverware."

"Nothing like gearing up for a night of dancing with a good meal." Aidan served himself a heaping plate of enchiladas and blew on a forkful to cool it before putting it in his mouth. "Damn, Wes, these are better than any Mexican restaurant. You are seriously going to make someone a great chef one day."

"I'm going to open my own restaurant one day," Wes corrected him. "And you'll all eat free because you knew me back when."

Jonah took a small helping from both pans, adding a dollop of guacamole to cool things off between bites.

"I definitely lucked out when it came to meeting you, Wes. I'd be eating fast food and ramen noodles if I was on my own."

"I might be eating ramen myself if you weren't here to help split the rent. It's a win-win situation all around."

It sure is, Jonah agreed silently. He'd had a small nest egg he'd saved up for the day he could leave Oktaha, though he'd planned to have a few more years to finish college and save more before that actually happened. Meeting Wes when he did had kept him from running out of money and possibly finding himself on the streets before he'd found a job in Dallas.

"Fabulous as always," Sammy declared before taking his empty plate to the dishwasher. "Aidan, be a doll and help Wes clean up while I take Jonah upstairs to get dressed."

"I can dress without help. I've been doing it for years," Jonah said with a grin.

"Yes, but left on your own you'd come down in overalls and a straw hat," Sammy teased. "I know we bought some decent clothes the last time we took you shopping. Let's go find them."

Despite Sammy's urging to add some color, Jonah selected his best pair of black jeans and a soft gray scoop-necked top. "The three of you have enough color to fill a box of Crayolas," he said with a laugh. "You don't need me to add to it."

"There is no such thing as too much color," Sammy countered, shaking his head as they walked back downstairs. "But I suppose I can bear to be seen with you in this. Aidan, Wes, let's get going."

Because Jonah didn't drink much, he was usually the designated driver for their nights out, though they took Aidan's Nissan since the four of them couldn't all fit in Jonah's truck. Wes suggested they try Echo, a new club that recently opened on Davis Street. It wasn't strictly a gay club, though like nearly all the businesses in Bishop Arts, it was definitely queer friendly. Jonah preferred staying in the neighborhood as opposed to visiting one of the larger gay bars on Cedar Springs, which seemed to him to cater to an older and more desperate-feeling clientele the one time he'd tried going there when he first arrived in the city.

Echo turned out to be a small building with a lively bar and a large dance floor. Loud house music pulsed with enough bass to echo in Jonas's chest, making him wonder if that's what gave the place its name. As he'd expected, there seemed to be as many mixed-sex as single-sex couples. Aidan headed to the bar to get drinks while Wes and Sammy snagged a high-top table along one of the walls. Before they had a chance to sit, someone called Wes's name, and he walked over to greet a friend at another table. Sammy caught Jonah's arm and pulled him out onto the dance floor. Aidan joined them as soon as he dropped the drinks at their table, and Wes and the friend he'd stopped to talk with followed a few minutes later.

Jonah enjoyed dancing, and for the first few songs he just let himself move to the music. Before too long, though, the night followed a predictable pattern. Sammy and Aidan soon had their arms wrapped around each other, not interested in dancing with anyone else. Wes was a social butterfly; he seemed to know at least half the people there and had a different partner for every song. When the heat from the dance floor got to be a bit much, Jonah returned to their table and took a grateful drink from the sweating glass of tonic water and lime Aidan had ordered him.

"Here alone?" someone asked.

Jonah turned toward a tall, dark-haired guy with even more muscles than Aidan. He thought it was an odd question when there were clearly three other drinks on the table, but he shook his head. "No, my friends are still dancing."

"Want to dance with me?"

Jonah really wanted to rest for a minute and finish his drink, but it felt rude to turn the guy down. "Sure."

It was too loud to carry on a conversation on the dance floor, but after several songs Jonah could feel sweat running down the back of his neck. He pointed toward the table, and his new friend followed. "I'm Jonah," he introduced himself when they got there.

"Nick," the other man offered in response. "Can I get you another drink?"

"Just tonic with lime. I'm the designated driver tonight," Jonah explained when the guy raised an eyebrow. He returned with a fresh drink for Jonah and something that looked like a rum and Coke for himself. Jonah sipped warily, scolding himself at his relief when the drink didn't contain any alcohol.

Nick, it turned out, was a personal trainer at a local gym. The noise level made it hard to hold a conversation, and it was easier to just follow Nick back onto the dance floor when they'd finished their drinks.

After another hour or so, Jonah was more than ready to head home, though since his three friends still seemed to be enjoying themselves, he was resigned to waiting for them. He excused himself to use the restroom, but when he came out, Nick was waiting in the hallway.

"What do you say we find somewhere a little more private?" he asked.

"I can't leave—I told you, I came with friends, and I'm driving."

"Guess we'll have to get to know each other better right here, then." Nick pulled Jonah by the arm, turning him until he was pinned between the wall and Nick's hard body. He worked a hand under the hem of Jonah's shirt and lowered his head as if to kiss him.

"Sorry, not interested." Jonah twisted his head and tried to squirm away, but he couldn't get free of Nick's grasp. He pushed forward, but Nick easily pressed him back against the wall. Jonah was considering elbowing him in the ribs when Wes's voice sounded behind Nick.

"Is this guy bothering you, babe?"

Nick stepped back, startled, and raised his hands. "Oh, hey, sorry. He didn't say anything about being taken."

Jonah didn't much care for the implication that he was a possession to be claimed, but it got Nick to take off, and that was what mattered. He pulled down his shirt and gave Wes a crooked smile. "Thanks. I don't think he was really dangerous, but I appreciate the help."

"Why didn't you just tell him to fuck off?"

"I tried, but he wasn't listening, and I didn't want to make a scene." He would have if things had gone much further, but his parents had taught him it was rude to make a spectacle of himself. Which was one of the reasons he'd wound up leaving Oktaha sooner than planned.

"If someone's doing something you don't want, go ahead and make the biggest scene you can. Shout, yell, knee him in the nuts if you have to." Wes pulled him into a hug. "Listen, do you want to head home? I can come back for Aidan and Sammy later."

"No." Jonah took a deep breath. "When you fall off a horse, you have to get right back on. I'm not letting one jerk ruin the night."

"Damn straight!" Wes gave him another squeeze and led him back onto the dance floor.

Chapter Four

LINC wasn't in the office on Monday, though Jonah hadn't expected him to be. He usually spent two or three days in a row in Dallas, depending on the amount of paperwork that needed action in any given week, and the rest of the time at the ranch. Jonah knew he'd planned to hold meetings with several more of the drillers who'd sent proposals to take over Courtwright Energy's leases, but after the outcome of last week's meetings, Jonah hadn't bothered to even open the calendar app on his computer. He knew his boss well enough to be sure he wouldn't approve of the drilling methods used by any of the other prospective bidders.

Instead Jonah spent the day researching the options for more environmentally friendly methods of natural gas recovery. It was quite an education. The Barnett

Shale, which underlay the Broken Spoke and more than 5,000 square miles of central and west Texas, was by some accounts the largest onshore natural gas field in the US. The problem was that the Shale's easily accessed oil and gas reserves had already been drilled. The gas trapped between the thick layers of rock that gave the formation its name was harder to extract, and hydraulic fracturing, horizontal drilling, and acidizing all had their drawbacks. Jonah made notes of the few firms he could find that seemed open to alternative methods to fracking, then composed a short document with some information about each and links to their web pages. He'd let Linc look it over whenever he came in and decide whether he wanted Jonah to set up face-to-face meetings with any of them.

He'd gotten so engaged in his research that he was surprised to notice it was after four by the time he had the memo finished. Monday and Wednesday were his class nights for the economics course he was taking at the downtown community college campus. On the way there, he stopped for a quick sandwich at Cindi's Deli across from Union Station—and, coincidentally, just a few blocks from Reunion Tower. He wondered whether Melissa had forgiven Linc for missing her celebratory dinner at Five Sixty. She'd probably be returning home today from the Tulsa rodeo and would see the bracelet Jonah'd had delivered. *I'd certainly never be able to stay angry at Linc for working too hard*, he thought, but then, he wasn't the one dating him. Shaking his head at his daydreams, he politely refused the older waitress who offered to refill his iced tea and walked to the counter to pay his bill, leaving a nice tip on the table on his way out. He knew how hard Wes worked for his tips and would always do his best to reward friendly service.

Class was challenging, and he enjoyed the discussion his teacher prompted among the students on how the various economic theories they were studying viewed the current business climate. He felt good about being able to contribute to the conversation based on his experience working for Linc. After making a note of the readings for Wednesday night's class, he said good night to a few of the classmates he'd gotten to know by virtue of sitting near them and headed home.

It wasn't until midmorning on Wednesday that Linc showed up at the office, smiling.

"You look like you had a good weekend," Jonah said, smiling back.

"Melissa really loved the bracelet," Linc answered.

"Your girlfriend must appreciate your good taste."

"I haven't got a girlfriend. I'm gay," Jonah was horrified to hear himself say. *Why the hell did I tell him that now?* It's not that he was hiding it—he'd come out of the closet and was never going back—but he watched Linc closely, a little afraid of how he'd react.

"Are you?" Linc replied with as little concern as if Jonah had told him his hair was brown. "Then I hope your boyfriend appreciates you."

"No boyfriend either at the moment." Jonah breathed a silent sigh of relief that his being gay didn't seem to make a bit of difference to his boss. He hadn't really expected Linc to be a homophobe, but then he hadn't expected it of the people he'd thought were his friends back in Oktaha either.

It seemed to Jonah that Linc glanced at him a bit speculatively at that comment, but luckily he didn't follow up on it. "I found several sources for organic feed and left the pricing information on your desk," Jonah said, happy to steer the subject from his social life—or lack of it—back to business. "Let me know which one you prefer, and I'll contact them about a reserve order. And none of the other bidders for the gas leases are big on environmental protection. I found a few other firms you might want to consider. They're smaller companies, for the most part, without as many years of experience, but they seem to have good track records so far. There's info on your desk about that too."

Linc leaned forward, resting his hands on the edge of Jonah's desk. This close, Jonah could smell a crisp, citrusy scent that wasn't strong enough to be aftershave or cologne. *It must be the soap he uses*, he thought, the idea bringing a flush of heat to his cheeks.

"Whatever I pay you, it isn't enough," Linc said. "Effective today you're getting a ten percent raise."

"I—thank you, Mr. Courtwright," Jonah stammered. He would have been satisfied just with the warm smile and the look of pride in his boss's hazel eyes.

Linc raised an eyebrow. "I've asked you before to please call me Linc."

Jonah nodded. "Thank you… Linc. That's very generous."

"You earn every penny of it. It would never occur to most people to take the initiative the way you do." Linc held his gaze a moment longer and then straightened. "Guess I'd better take a look at those files you put together for me. I can't have you getting too far ahead of me, can I?"

JONAH spent the rest of the afternoon dealing with e-mail and updating the latest sales statistics into the master cattle records. Linc didn't stick his head out of the inner office until almost four thirty.

"Jonah, I think these drilling firms you researched show real promise. Can you set up meetings with them for me as soon as possible?"

"Can it wait until tomorrow morning?" Jonah asked guiltily. Here he'd just been given a big raise, and the first time his boss—Linc—asked him to do something, he had to ask if he could delay it. "I have class tonight, and I'll just have time to grab some fast food on the way to make it before it starts."

Linc grimaced. "I meant for you to schedule the meetings for as soon as possible, not that you had to do it immediately. Go ahead, go to class. I'll shut down your computer before I leave. Go!"

He made shooing motions with his hands, and Jonah had to grin.

"If that's how you herd cattle, I hate to tell you, but you're doing it wrong." Jonah reached under his desk to grab his backpack and hide his face. He didn't know what had come over him today, but he couldn't seem to control his mouth.

To his relief, Linc was laughing when he stood up. "I'll have to get you to the ranch someday to show you how it's done. Now go on to class. Git!"

Jonah wasn't sure how he made it to class—he didn't even bother stopping at Cindi's for a sandwich on the way—and he couldn't have said later what the lecture was about. He spent the entire time replaying the two conversations with Linc in his mind.

"I GOT a raise!" Jonah announced to Wes when he stopped at Prism after class finally let out. "Linc gave me a ten percent increase!"

"Awesome!" Wes reached across the bar to bump knuckles with Jonah. "I'm glad he appreciates all the extra work you put in for him. It's not like you're hourly and get overtime when you stay there late."

"I'm just happy that he thinks I'm doing a good job, considering how little I knew about oil and gas leases when I started. But it's really interesting, you know?"

"If you say so." Wes set a cocktail glass in front of him. "Here, try this and tell me what you think."

Jonah took a sip. "Wow, that's really good. What's in it? I taste peach… and ginger?"

"Peach-infused vodka, ginger beer, lime juice, and mint. I call it 'Just Peachy.'"

"It's great, but I'd better order something to eat too. I didn't have time for supper before class, and if I drink this on an empty stomach, you'll be carrying me home."

"Try the artichoke chicken salad sandwich with zucchini chips," Wes suggested. "I don't know what Manny puts on the zucchini besides parmesan cheese, but they're fantastic."

"And I can pay for it too," Jonah crowed.

"Just don't tell Sammy you got a raise," Wes warned. "He'll want you to spend it all on new clothes."

THURSDAY morning Jonah arrived in the office to an e-mail from Linc's ranch foreman, Ford Slater, to let him know they were selling off a number of breeder cows to another ranch. It took him all morning and half the afternoon to update the computer records of the cows being sold. Linc stopped in during the morning to tell Jonah about the sale but left shortly after to take Melissa to lunch. She would be leaving soon for a series of rodeo competitions on the West Coast that would keep her on the road for the next several weeks. Jonah grabbed a prepackaged carton of cheese and crackers from the cafeteria on the ground floor of their building and ate at his desk, trying not to feel envious of Melissa for getting to spend the time with Linc.

When he finally finished updating the herd records, Jonah placed small orders for winter feed with two of the organic suppliers Linc had selected, wanting to get a feel for the quality of each. He noted the expenses in the ranch's budget spreadsheet and then turned to the file on environmentally sensitive natural gas drillers. Linc had made notes in the margin next to each of the entries and scrawled across the bottom, *Set up meetings with all of them ASAP*.

Jonah opened the calendar program on his computer and started making phone calls. Linc came back to the office at some point during the afternoon, but Jonah barely noticed, raising a hand to acknowledge his return and pointing to his headset to indicate he was tied up. Linc nodded and went into the inner office, and Jonah worked on holding back his frustration at being repeatedly placed on hold and transferred around until he could reach the proper person at each company to schedule the meetings Linc had asked for.

When he had all the meetings scheduled for various dates within the next two weeks, updated the printouts with the correct contact information for each firm, and entered the information in the online contact and calendar databases, Jonah pulled off his headset and sat back with a sigh. His stomach rumbled, and he was shocked to discover when he looked at the clock on his monitor that it was nearly seven o'clock.

He was reviewing his notes about the dates of the various meetings to leave on Linc's desk when the door to the inner office opened and Linc came out. With all the hoops he'd had to jump through to set up the meetings, Jonah had forgotten he was there.

"What are you still doing here?" Linc asked, frowning.

"I was setting up those meetings you asked for," Jonah explained. "I didn't realize how many layers I'd have to go through to find the right person to talk with at each firm. It took longer than I'd expected, and I guess I lost track of time."

"Even with a raise, I don't pay you enough to put in eleven-hour days," Linc said.

Jonah's stomach chose that moment to grumble again, loudly enough that Linc clearly heard it.

"That does it. Shut down your computer. I'm taking you out to dinner."

"You don't have to do that," Jonah protested automatically. *Shut up and go with him,* something inside him insisted. *You were jealous of Melissa getting to have lunch with him. Let him take you to dinner!*

"Of course I don't have to. I want to." Linc leaned over Jonah's desk, close enough to let him catch another hint of that citrusy scent, and pushed the button to turn off his monitor. "Now grab your backpack and whatever else you need and let's go. I'm starving."

Chapter Five

"SO, what do you have a taste for?" Linc asked as they rode the elevator to the parking garage.

"Uh… anything?" Jonah grinned. "I had some cheese and crackers for lunch, so at this point my stomach will be happy just as long as I put something in it. There's a deli a few blocks away where I stop for dinner before class sometimes?" As soon as he suggested it, he second-guessed himself. Cindi's food was good and the portions were large, but Linc was surely used to more elegant dining. "It's nothing fancy," he added quickly.

"You deserve more than a deli sandwich," Linc said. "There's a steakhouse not far from here. We can get a good meal there. The place Melissa picked for lunch served rabbit food. I could go for a nice thick steak myself."

Jonah could have done without the reminder of Linc's girlfriend. For just a moment he'd allowed himself to think Linc had asked him out because he wanted to spend more time with him. *He just needs to eat and probably doesn't want to do it alone*, Jonah told himself. *Don't try to turn it into something it's not.* "I'm not exactly dressed for anywhere fancy," he said instead, looking down at his usual work outfit of khaki pants and a short-sleeved shirt.

"Neither am I," Linc answered with a grin.

There wasn't a thing wrong with his well-cut jeans and western shirt, to Jonah's mind.

"I get enough of fancy places with Melissa. No one will say a word about the way we're dressed." He paused when they stepped out of the elevator on the floor with parking spaces reserved for Linc's office. "Do you want to go in my truck or follow me? I'll be happy to bring you back here when we're done if you'd rather not drive."

The idea of sitting next to Linc on the bench seat of his truck was appealing—maybe too appealing. Jonah shook his head. "I can follow you. That way we can both just head home when we're done."

"Works for me," Linc answered. "The restaurant's just down Market Street at Ross—the Y.O. Ranch Steakhouse."

"I know where that is," Jonah said. "It's just past where I take my class at El Centro."

"I'll see you there, then." Linc climbed into his truck and started the engine.

Jonah spent the short drive to the restaurant telling himself not to let one dinner go to his head. Sure, the more he got to know Lincoln Courtwright as a person and not just as his employer, the more he liked him, but he couldn't jeopardize his job by giving away any indication of his attraction. Linc might not have a problem with Jonah being gay, but that didn't mean he'd feel the same if he thought Jonah was coming on to him.

The steakhouse was located in an old brick building in the West End Historic District. Jonah found a place to park on the street and walked the short distance back to the restaurant. Linc was already waiting inside.

"It will be a few minutes for a table. Would you like something from the bar while we wait?" Linc asked.

"I'm not much of a drinker," Jonah said. "Wes— that's my roommate—he works at a restaurant and is always getting me to try the new drinks he comes up with because he says if I like them, anyone will."

"We'll wait until we're seated, thanks," Linc told the hostess who was hovering nearby.

Jonah took the time while they waited to look around. The inside of the restaurant was warm and welcoming, with exposed brick walls, high beamed ceilings, and cream-colored wooden pillars. The people he could see at the tables were a mix of businessmen, couples, and tourists, all of them dressed as casually as he and Linc, if not more so. Feeling a bit more relaxed, he was trying to find a topic to talk about that might interest Linc when the hostess told them their table was ready.

Linc gestured for Jonah to precede him, so he followed the hostess up a few stairs to a section of tables along the wall perpendicular to the bar. "Enjoy your meal, gentlemen," she said as she handed them their menus.

Jonah had barely opened his and glanced at the prices—not as outrageous as he'd been afraid they might be, though certainly more than he'd spend on a meal for himself—when a waiter approached them. "Good evening, gentleman. Welcome to the Y.O. Ranch Steakhouse. I'm Hector, and I'll be your server this evening. Are you familiar with our restaurant?"

"I am, but my guest…?" Linc glanced at Jonah, who shook his head.

"You're in for a treat, then," Hector said with a smile. "All our beef is USDA Prime, and our steaks are hand carved in house. We're also known for our wild game selections, most of which are raised on the ranch itself. I'll give you a few minutes to explore the menu, but in the meantime, can I get you something to drink?"

"Just an iced tea, please," Jonah said.

Linc asked for a Shiner, and the waiter hurried to the bar to place their order.

"So what looks good to you?" Linc asked when Jonah returned to studying the menu.

"I've never had some of these game items," Jonah answered. "I had venison once, and I didn't much care for it. It was a bit dry, though maybe that was the way it was prepared."

"You might like the buffalo filet," Linc suggested. "They do a good job with it here."

When Hector returned with their drinks, Jonah took Linc's suggestion and ordered the filet medium rare. Linc ordered a sirloin, also medium rare. "I guess we have something in common," Linc observed with a smile that made Jonah's insides heat up.

"Is the Broken Spoke anything like the Y.O.?" he asked, needing to distract himself from Linc's all too arousing expression.

"Well, we don't raise anything more exotic than some chickens for the eggs," Linc said. "My dad played around with raising beefalo—that's a cross between a domestic bull and a bison cow—back in the early eighties, but there was never much of a market for it." He took a drink from his longneck, having declined the glass Hector offered when he served them. "The Spoke has actually been around a bit longer than the Y.O. The Courtwright who founded it bought the original land just after the Civil War, though it's been added to several times since."

"That's a heritage to be proud of," Jonah said. "Genealogy is one of Wes's hobbies. He's researched his family tree on Ancestry.com back to early England and Scotland."

Linc frowned, though Jonah couldn't think of anything he'd said to cause it. "You'd have to ask my father's second wife, Eloise, about the family history."

Jonah thought it was odd that Linc didn't refer to her as his stepmother, but Linc continued before he could pursue the niggling impression.

"She's one of those people who marry into a family and takes more of an interest in its background than the family does itself. She has a family tree and a coat of arms and everything hanging on the walls in the big living room."

"The big living room as opposed to the small one?" Jonah teased. "How many living rooms do you have, anyway?"

"Hell, I don't know. The house is like the ranch—it kind of sprawls, because over time different Courtwrights added on to it as the family grew. There's plenty of space, that's for sure."

It sounded so different from the compact three-bedroom farmhouse Jonah grew up in. Before he could ask another question, their meals arrived, and they spent a few minutes cutting into their perfectly cooked steaks.

"Good?" Linc asked as Jonah took a bite and the rich flavor exploded on his tongue.

"Fantastic," Jonah answered. Not that it was likely to be something he'd have the chance to enjoy again, so he'd focus on savoring this meal and this night.

"Great. So tell me a bit about yourself. You're not from Dallas, are you?"

"Is it that easy to tell?" Jonah asked, wondering what he'd done to give himself away.

"Most of the people in Dallas aren't from Dallas," Linc said. "If I had to guess, I'd say either west Texas or Oklahoma."

"Oklahoma," Jonah confirmed. "A little town near Muskogee called Oktaha."

Linc nodded, though Jonah doubted he was familiar with it. Oktaha was too small—fewer than four hundred residents, and that was counting all the farms and ranches for miles around it. "What brought you here to Dallas?"

Jonah paused, weighing what he wanted to tell Linc. *He already knows I'm gay*, he thought. *And it's not like I have anything to be ashamed of.* "Oktaha's pretty much in the middle of nowhere. My best friend, Caylee Lynch, and I always swore we'd get out of there as soon as we could and see some of the world. Our plan was to finish college and then head to Dallas or somewhere like it to find jobs." He paused to sip his tea. "Caylee started dating Jack Ballinger—his dad owns the biggest cattle operation in the area. My mom and Caylee's mom were best friends growing up, and they'd always had this dream that one day their children would get married to each other. Caylee's mom died when she was ten, but Mom has never really given up on the idea. She started in on telling me how I needed to woo Caylee if I wanted to keep her. I finally got tired of it and told her that as much as I love Caylee like a sister, I was never going to ask her to marry me because I'm gay."

"How did she take it?" Linc asked after a moment.

"They didn't kick me out or anything, if that's what you're thinking. She wasn't thrilled—she told me it was just a phase I was going through. My dad didn't say much, though he rarely does, but I know they think homosexuality is a sin." Jonah pushed around some of the vegetables on his plate. "Not that I ever did anything to act on it. Caylee knew, of course, but there isn't anyone else in Oktaha who's gay, at least that I know of, and no one I was attracted to, anyway. Then one day between classes—I went to Connors State in Warner, which is the closest college to Oktaha—I was sitting in the cafeteria, and a guy from my English class came and sat with me. He said he'd noticed me in class and was wondering if I'd like to go out with him sometime. I'm not sure how he knew I was gay, but we were just talking, and one of the other people from Oktaha who took classes there too must have overheard us, or maybe just saw us together and took a guess. Anyway, before I knew it, it was all over town that I was gay."

Linc's expression was too guarded for Jonah to decipher. "Hard to keep a secret in a small town. I gather not everyone was supportive?"

"I got hassled, yeah." Jonah didn't especially want to remember the cold shoulders and insults he'd gotten from people he'd thought of as friends. He especially didn't want to relive the day Jack Ballinger had taken him aside and told him he didn't want his girl hanging around with a fucking faggot. He'd meant to tell Caylee what a jerk she was dating, but when he'd tried to bring up the subject, Caylee all but gushed about how sweet Jack was, and Jonah couldn't bear to disillusion her. "Eventually I decided it wasn't worth putting up with it, so I left for Dallas a little sooner than I'd planned." He'd asked Caylee to come with him, but she'd wanted to see where her relationship with Jack might go. Jonah hoped once he wasn't around to be a target for Jack's hatefulness, he'd be the man Caylee thought he was.

"Did you know anyone in Dallas when you got here?" Linc asked.

"No, but I had a bit of a nest egg I'd saved up from working left over after I paid for classes. It wasn't as big as it would have been if I'd stayed two more years, but it was enough to get me started. I looked up gay-friendly neighborhoods on the Internet and found a hotel I could afford in Oak Lawn while I started looking for a job. The neighborhood was louder and busier than I was used to, but then I found Bishop Arts. It's got much more of a small-town feeling—nearly all the businesses are independently owned, not chains, and lots of them have rainbow flags in the windows and put bowls of water on their doorsteps for customers' dogs."

"I've never been there, but I'm going to have to check it out," Linc said.

"Anyway, one day I was having lunch in a little sandwich shop and looking through the paper for job listings. I got to talking with the waiter, and before I knew it, he'd gotten my life story out of me—kind of like you," Jonah said with a smile. "That's how I met Wes. By the end of the meal, he told me he'd been looking for someone to share the rent in the townhouse he lived in and asked me to take a look at it. I met the two guys who lived in the other half of the building, Sammy and Aidan, and Aidan gave me a lead with the temp agency he'd worked for before he found his current job. And that led to my working with Jennifer on your cattle registry update, and here we are."

"And I'm very glad you are," Linc said.

Jonah was surprised to realize they'd both finished their steaks while he was talking.

"Would you like some dessert?"

"Not for me, thanks. I don't usually eat this big a meal this late at night."

Linc settled the check, thanking Hector for his service, and they stood to walk out of the restaurant. The sun had set, cooling the air slightly, though the heat still rose from the sidewalk. "I had a good time," Linc said. "We should do this again some night."

"Next time will be my treat," Jonah answered. "I did just get a big raise, after all."

Linc gave him another one of those heart-melting smiles. "So you did. Have a safe drive home, Jonah."

"You too. Will I see you in the office tomorrow?"

"No, I think I'm going to head back to the ranch in the morning, make sure the cows we sold get delivered safely. Have a good weekend."

"Thanks, you too." Jonah walked to his truck and started the drive home, telling himself not to read too much into Linc's words. *He was just being polite. Don't get your hopes up over something that's just Linc being friendly.* Still, he couldn't keep from smiling all the way home.

Chapter Six

EVEN though Linc wasn't in the office on Friday, Jonah felt his presence there all day. He'd be pulling up a file or reading an e-mail, and suddenly he'd remember the warmth in Linc's eyes while he listened to Jonah talk about leaving home, or the way everything seemed to brighten when he laughed. He'd go into Linc's office to drop a piece of mail on his desk and swear he could catch a lingering hint of his citrusy scent.

This has to stop, he told himself when he realized he'd had the ranch budget open on his computer for ten minutes and hadn't entered a single invoice. It was just a business dinner, even if they hadn't spent any time actually talking about business—Linc's way of thanking him for his efforts at work. He'd be foolish to imagine it was anything more, especially with the bill for Melissa's bracelet sitting right in front of him. He'd do better to convince himself to be happy with Linc's friendship, since it was the most he was going to get.

Wes had a rare Friday night off from work, so Jonah drove home to find him chopping vegetables in the kitchen. "I thought I'd make a chicken stir-fry for dinner," he said. "It won't take long to cook up—I was waiting for you to get home to start."

"Sounds delicious. I'll make some rice," Jonah offered.

"So you were late getting in last night," Wes said casually after Jonah had loaded the rice cooker and plugged it in.

Jonah felt his cheeks turn red and hoped Wes would attribute it to his bending over to get into the lower cabinet where they stored the appliances. "We worked late, and Linc took me out to dinner after we finished up."

The pan sizzled as Wes dumped the chicken into it. "Dinner, huh?" he said. "I'm guessing he didn't just buy you a burger or some pizza."

"We went to a steakhouse near the office."

Wes just looked at him, not even watching the pan as he tossed the contents to sear them evenly.

"What?" Jonah asked.

"You tell me—you're the one blushing."

"I'm not blushing. It was just a friendly dinner. I told him I'd take him out next time." Jonah frowned. "Though I don't know where I could take him. The only restaurants I know near the office are fast-food places or diners. I guess I'll have to google what other nice restaurants there are downtown."

Wes poured the chicken into a bowl and added the vegetables to the pan. "There's the wine walk next weekend. You could ask him to that."

"I don't know… I'm not even sure he likes wine. He just had a beer with dinner."

"What rich guy doesn't like wine?" Wes asked, then tasted a pea pod and poured some soy sauce into the pan before tossing the chicken back in. "Besides, I'll be working Friday night—it's great for tips—so I'd get a chance to meet him."

"That's an argument not to invite him," Jonah retorted, smiling to take the sting from his teasing. "Besides, he usually spends weekends at the ranch. I'm not sure he'd want to stay in town just to go on a wine walk with me."

"You won't know unless you ask him, will you?" Wes said. "This is almost done—grab some plates and let's eat."

BY the time Linc came into the office on Tuesday, Jonah had rehearsed a dozen different ways to ask about Friday night. If the rules of etiquette his mother had drilled into him didn't require that he reciprocate an invitation as soon as possible, he'd be tempted to forget the whole thing. But she'd raised him to be polite, and even though she'd never know if he didn't follow through, he'd still feel guilty about not doing the right thing.

"Good morning, Jonah." Linc greeted him with the smile Jonah always found devastating. "Anything important I need to know about?"

"The schedule for the meetings with the natural gas drillers is on your calendar, there's an inquiry from a new distributor who wants to carry Broken Spoke beef, and would you like to go on a wine walk in Bishop Arts Friday night?" Blurting it out like that had *not* been one of the strategies he'd practiced, but Linc's smile just grew.

"A wine walk? How about you come into my office and tell me about it?"

Jonah followed Linc into his inner sanctum and sank into a chair while Linc settled behind his desk. "A few times a year, the local merchants sponsor a wine walk for charity. You pay fifteen or twenty dollars for a glass, and the shops and restaurants have different kinds of wines you can sample. I think the money for this one is going to Jonathan's Place, a center that helps abused and abandoned children."

"It sounds like a wonderful cause," Linc commented.

"It lasts from six to nine, and if we get there early, I thought we could have dinner at Prism—the restaurant my roommate, Wes, works at—though there are a lot of other restaurants in the area if you'd rather try something else. And then we can walk around to see the different shops. If you're interested, that is. I know you usually go home to the ranch over the weekend, and I'll understand if you don't want to stay in the city, or if it's not something that appeals to you, or—"

"Jonah, take a breath." Linc chuckled. "I'd love to go with you."

"You would?" Jonah realized how immature that sounded, but it seemed every time he talked to Linc about anything but business, his mouth starting flying on autopilot.

"Yes, I would. After hearing you talk about Bishop Arts last week, I'd like to see the area. And I'm always happy to support a good cause, especially when it's something local. So it's a date."

If only that were true, Jonah thought and immediately told himself not to go there. "I'll put it on your calendar so you don't forget."

"You do that," Linc said. "Now how about you tell me about this new distributor you mentioned?"

THE rest of the week felt to Jonah like it flew past. Linc was in the office every day, though that didn't mean Jonah saw all that much of him. After some lengthy phone calls, Linc apparently worked out an agreement with the firm that wanted to buy beef from the ranch. He met with his attorney to iron out the contract details and also spent time on the phone with his foreman to discuss the logistics of the sale. Jonah felt a bit guilty that Linc could have had that discussion in person if he wasn't staying in town, but not guilty enough to dim his anticipation for Friday night. Linc made sure Jonah left early enough on Wednesday to have time for dinner before class, and he brought him a burger from the cafeteria on Thursday when he'd gotten caught up in handling the end-of-month budget entries and worked through lunch. Jonah tried hard not to let the attention go to his head. Melissa was on the West Coast WPRA tour, so maybe Linc was feeling a bit lonely.

At four o'clock Friday afternoon, Linc came out of his office and leaned over Jonah's desk. "Turn that computer off. The work week is officially over."

"I don't know," Jonah answered. "My boss is pretty demanding. I wouldn't want him to think I was ducking out early."

"Yeah, I've heard he can be a real hardass."

Jonah chuckled, though he didn't think there was a darned thing wrong with Linc's ass. He wondered how Linc would react if he said that but decided he was afraid to find out.

"We'll risk it anyway," Linc said. "C'mon, let's go. I'll follow you this time."

IT took a little longer than usual to find parking, probably because of all the people coming for the wine walk. Prism was one of the sites selling glasses, so Jonah paid the hostess for two before she seated them at a four-top that seemed to be the only empty table in the restaurant. "It's a good thing we got here early," Jonah said. "They don't take reservations, and it's a small enough place that it fills up fast."

Before Linc could answer, Wes came over to the table, holding a tray with two cocktail glasses. "I know this is a wine walk, but I have a new drink I want you to try first. I call it 'Get Lucky.'" He winked at Jonah, who hoped fervently Linc didn't see it. "I'm Wes, and you must be Linc." He wiped his hand off on his jeans before offering it, and Linc shook it.

The contrast between the two was almost funny— Wes in distressed black jeans and a T-shirt that announced "Sleeping with the Bartender Might Not Get You Free Drinks, But It's Worth a Shot," the hot-pink color contrasting vividly with his blue spiked hair; Linc in a denim shirt, blue jeans, and boots, his hair still brushing his collar…. Jonah really needed to remember to schedule him for a haircut.

"Pleased to meet you," Linc said. "I've heard a lot about you from Jonah."

Jonah supposed he should be grateful that Wes didn't roll his eyes. "Likewise," he said. "I've got to get back to work, but try the drinks. It's cucumber-infused

rum with lime juice and mint. Should get your night off
to a good start." He gave Jonah a hug before heading
back to the bar.

Linc raised his glass and held it toward Jonah's.
"To tonight," he said with a smile.

Jonah touched his glass to Linc's and took a sip.
The drink was crisp and refreshing, but not enough to
quell the heat spreading inside him. "The menu's on
the board," he said quickly, turning to read the nightly
specials. "They have tuna steak tonight—that's always
good—and, ooh, buffalo mac and cheese! That's my
favorite thing on their menu. Not that they actually
have a menu, but I always order that when it shows up."

"Tuna sounds good," Linc started to say when
someone pulled out a chair beside him.

"It's a good thing we saw you sitting here, or we
never would have gotten a table," Aidan said, seating
Sammy before coming around the table to sit in the last
chair. "You don't mind if we join you, do you?"

Though sorely tempted to answer otherwise, Jonah
said, "No, of course not. This is my boss, Lincoln
Courtwright. Linc, these are my friends Aidan Jacobs
and Samuel Tanner. They live in the other half of the
building with Wes and me."

"You must be the one who owns the big ranch,"
Sammy said. "You sure look like a real cowboy, not
one of those little boys playing dress-up. 'All hat and
no buckle,' my momma would say."

Jonah wondered what Linc thought of Sammy's
rainbow-patterned shirt over slim red slacks or Aidan's
violet scooped-neck top and rolled-up jeans. Personally
he was about ready for the floor to open and swallow
him up.

"I do own a ranch," Linc admitted. "I even wear a hat at times when I'm there."

Aidan broke into a laugh. "I'll bet you've got a few buckles too. You don't keep a build like that riding a desk."

Jonah tried desperately to squash the images that raised and was pathetically grateful when the waitress came to take their orders.

LINC invited Sammy and Aidan to join them on the wine walk when they finished dinner, and after stopping at the bar to say good-bye to Wes—and for Jonah to notice Linc slipping a large bill into the tip jar—they walked out onto Bishop Avenue.

"Most of the shops are here or on Davis Street," Jonah said. "We can just stroll and stop in anywhere that catches your attention."

"You have to take him to Dude, Sweet Chocolate," Sammy insisted. "Best truffles you've ever had in your life."

"And Emporium Pies later, if the line's not too long," Aidan added.

"He's not kidding about the line," Jonah said, pointing down the block to where a queue of people spilled out the door of what looked like a small cottage and stretched halfway down the block. "They only make six or seven kinds a season, but they're incredible."

"We'll definitely stop there before we leave," Linc promised. "But for now, lead on. I'm in your hands."

Jonah smothered a groan and started down the block. It was going to be a long night.

Chapter Seven

GIVEN his almost constant state of embarrassment at supper, Jonah was surprised at how much he enjoyed the rest of the evening. The weather was still as hot as could be expected in early September, but the trees that lined the streets provided shade from the lowering sun, and a slight breeze augmented the air-conditioning seeping out from more than a few open shop doors. Whether Wes's drink had been stronger than it tasted, or it was the wine on top of it—though Jonah was careful to limit himself to a small taste at each stop—he found himself relaxing as they walked from store to store. Linc didn't appear at all put out by Sammy and Aidan joining them, chuckling at even the most outrageous of Sammy's comments and contributing some stories about incidents at the ranch that had them all laughing.

He seemed charmed by the variety of clothing stores, salons, antiques sellers, and gift shops they walked in and out of, even buying a box of truffles when they stopped at the chocolatier toward the end of the walk. Jonah couldn't help but wonder if it was a gift for Melissa when she returned from her rodeo tour.

That return was still a couple of weeks away, and that was the only explanation Jonah could come up with for how much more time Linc seemed to be spending with him when he was in the office. He'd started inviting Jonah to join him for lunch—though Jonah had only agreed on the condition that they each paid for themselves—or bringing something to Jonah on those days he was too busy to stop what he was working on at lunchtime. On the nights he had classes, Linc made sure Jonah left the office with plenty of time to stop somewhere for dinner first. He'd even mentioned that Jonah should come out to the ranch sometime soon so he could get a firsthand look at both the cattle and the energy operations. Jonah kept telling himself not to read anything more into it than friendship. He knew Melissa had called several times when Linc was in the office, since about the only time Linc closed his door was to talk with her. Jonah made himself go out clubbing with his friends each weekend and danced and got into conversations with several guys he met, though none of them struck even a spark of the heat Linc could generate with one careless smile.

Two weeks after the wine walk, Linc was meeting with one of the environmentally focused natural gas drillers Jonah had scheduled when Melissa breezed into the office. Jonah didn't follow rodeo and had no idea whether she had done well or not in her events, but judging by the wide smile on her face, he assumed she was happy with her results.

"I've come to take Linc to lunch. Let him know I'm here," she said, sweeping her long blonde hair behind her shoulders. Jonah noticed she was wearing the sapphire tennis bracelet he'd ordered, with a sleek wrap dress in shades of blue that brought out the color of her eyes. A silver belt accented her slim waist, and the split at the crossover hem drew attention to her long legs and grey ostrich-skin boots.

"Was Mr. Courtright expecting you?" Jonah asked, knowing full well he wasn't. Linc never made plans for the days he had important meetings scheduled, since he never knew whether they might run long and didn't want to risk cutting a promising discussion short.

"He knew I was getting back in town last night." Melissa said. "We had a long talk on the phone the night before"—Jonah had to blink to rid himself of the image of Linc lying in bed, the sheets wrapped around his legs but baring his chest, his husky voice murmuring to Melissa how much he'd missed her—"and I wanted to surprise him."

It certainly was a surprise, and not a welcome one, at least as far as Jonah was concerned. "I'm sorry, Ms. Cutler, but he's been in a meeting all morning. I don't know how much longer it will be before they're finished."

"Why don't you just call him and let him know I'm here?" Her proprietary smile seemed almost predatory. "I'm sure that will give him incentive to wrap things up quickly."

"Mr. Courtright has strict rules never to be interrupted during meetings." *You should know*, Jonah thought. *You've tried to get me to break them often enough when you call.* "If you'd like to wait, you could have a seat right over there." Jonah gestured toward the pair of upholstered chairs with a table holding a collection of *Working Ranch*, *Progressive Cattleman*, and *Beef* magazines between them. "Can I get you a cup of coffee or some water?"

Melissa looked at the door to Linc's office as if she were seriously considering yanking it open and dragging Linc out by his collar. Jonah cleared his throat, wondering if he was going to have to physically restrain her, but she gave an unhappy *hmppph* of breath and sat down heavily in one of the chairs. "Coffee, skim milk and two Splendas," she said as if she was ordering at a restaurant.

Jonah got up from his desk and crossed the waiting room to pop a pod into the Keurig machine, then checked the small refrigerator under the counter. As he expected, there were only a handful of individual cups of creamer, since Linc took his coffee black and Jonah seldom drank any at work. He fixed the coffee once it finished brewing and brought it over to Melissa. "I'm sorry, we don't have any skim milk, so I had to use half-and-half."

She looked up from checking her smartphone and nodded toward the table with a frown but didn't say anything. Jonah set the cup down and returned to his desk, hoping Linc's meeting would end soon.

Unfortunately Linc had no way of knowing about the growing tension in his outer office. Melissa drank her coffee and spent more time keying into her phone, but when half an hour had passed, she got up and started pacing. It was impossible for Jonah to concentrate on the e-mail he was trying to compose to Linc's accountant when every time Melissa crossed in front of him he worried she might barge in to Linc's office.

Nearly an hour passed before Linc's door finally opened and he and the representative from DrillTech Energy walked into the waiting room. Linc glanced from Melissa to Jonah, who shrugged, but he didn't immediately acknowledge her. "Thank you for your time, and you can expect to hear from me after I've completed my evaluations," he said, shaking hands with the sales rep. Not until the other man was out of the office did he turn to Melissa. "This is a pleasant surprise. I hope you weren't waiting for long?"

Melissa looked like she was about to explode. "I wouldn't have had to wait if your guard dog here had let you know as soon as I arrived. He kept me sitting here for over an hour—"

Linc broke in to Melissa's tirade. "Jonah is my administrative assistant, not my guard dog, and he did exactly what I've instructed him to do. If I'd known you were planning to stop by, I could have told you I had a meeting this morning that might run long." He took a deep breath and smiled, even if to Jonah it seemed a bit forced. "Why don't you let me take you out for a late lunch, and you can tell me all about the tour."

Melissa shook her head forcefully enough to set her hair flipping around her shoulders. "If you expect what we have to continue, we need to get a few things straight. He"—she pointed at Jonah, who lowered his eyes in embarrassment—"needs to learn that when I call, he puts me through to you. And you"—she pointed at Linc—"need to make a commitment that our relationship is your top priority. I'm tired of taking a backseat to your meetings and your cows and your 'assistant.'"

Jonah really didn't want to be in the middle of this confrontation, but Melissa was standing in front of the door with her hands on her hips, glaring at Linc, and until she moved he wouldn't be able to get around her to leave the office. He turned his chair away from them and tried to focus on his computer screen, but he couldn't block out Linc's voice, sounding cooler than he could ever remember hearing it.

"Just what kind of 'relationship' do you think we have?"

"We're going to get married, of course."

Melissa made it sound as if it were a foregone conclusion, and Jonah hoped neither of them was paying him any attention because he was sure he cringed. He didn't know if he'd be able to continue to work with Linc if having to deal with Melissa as Mrs. Courtwright was part of the job description.

Linc's voice was surprisingly calm. "I don't recall having asked you, Melissa."

Her laugh was brittle. "Well, it's just a matter of time, isn't it? A man doesn't give the kind of presents you do if he isn't serious."

Jonah tried to shrink into his desk chair. He couldn't believe this was happening. She was basing Linc's feelings on a few presents he hadn't even picked out for her? Oh hell, was this all his fault for doing his job too well? He was tempted to peek over his shoulder to see Linc's expression, but there was no way he wanted to draw their focus to himself.

"Melissa, we've had some good times together, but I thought you understood that was all it was." Melissa's breath caught, and Linc's voice gentled. "I'm sorry if I gave you the wrong impression, but you're looking for something more than I'm prepared to give. I think it might be best if we leave it at that."

"What?" Melissa all but screeched. "You think you can just drop me like this? You have no idea what you're throwing away, Lincoln Courtwright! I'm not going to let you get away with treating me this way. You think any other woman is going to want to date you when they hear what I have to say about you?"

Jonah wasn't sure how Linc managed to remain calm in the face of Melissa's vitriol.

"I don't really care what you have to say about me, Melissa. I think it's clear we're not looking for the same things. We'll both be happier if we don't see each other again."

"Happier?"

Jonah risked a quick glance over his shoulder. Melissa's face was so twisted with anger, it was hard to believe she was the same beautiful woman who'd entered the office, while Linc's expression might have been carved from stone.

"We'll see how happy you are when I let everyone know what you're really like. You'll care when people stop thinking you're God's gift to women and won't have anything to do with you. Then who'll buy your overpriced organic beef? The only way you'll get someone to sleep with you will be to bed down with your stupid cows!"

That shocked Jonah enough to spin his chair back around. He didn't know how Linc managed not to respond to her in kind. But whatever reaction Melissa was expecting to get from her tirade, Linc didn't give it to her. He simply reached around her to open the glass office door and held it politely. "I don't think we have anything else to say to each other, Melissa. You have a good day."

Melissa swung her arm and her palm connected to Linc's cheek with a solid slap. When even that didn't wring a reaction from him, she spun on her boot heels and stormed out of the office, muttering under her breath.

Linc turned to Jonah with a rueful smile. "Well, hell."

Chapter Eight

"I'M sorry," Jonah said, though he couldn't really be sorry Melissa was out of the picture. She'd shown her true colors with that immature tantrum, and Linc deserved someone much better. "I didn't mean to sit here and listen to your private business, but I was sort of stuck at my desk. I couldn't get around her to the door, or I would have gone to lunch and maybe you could have worked something out." *Even if I'm glad to see the last of her*, he added silently.

"I'm just sorry you had to witness it. I know it must have been awkward for you." Linc sighed. "Lunch sounds like a good idea. Let's get out of here and find somewhere to eat. My treat for making you sit through that."

Jonah didn't argue, even if he normally insisted on paying his own way. He figured Linc had dealt with enough confrontation for the day. "We could go to Cindi's. It's not far, and it's enough past normal lunchtime that it shouldn't be too crowded."

"I'll drive," Linc offered, and since Jonah didn't have a good reason to take both their trucks, he agreed. Despite its age, the interior of Linc's Ford was in good condition, Jonah observed when he took a seat in the cab. "I hope you don't mind if we just roll down the windows," Linc said as he maneuvered out of the parking garage. "The air-conditioning works, but it takes a while to cool down, and we'll be there before it does."

"It's fine," Jonah said, cranking his window open. "I spend so much time in air-conditioning that sometimes I like to just put the windows down and let the breeze blow through my hair, even if it's hot air."

"My dad called it 'four-forty air-conditioning,'" Linc said with a laugh. "Open all four windows and drive at least forty. Though with the truck I can only open three windows, counting the back one over the bed."

Jonah had a sudden image of driving down a country road with Linc, except in his mind he was sitting in the middle of the bench seat with Linc's arm around him, not as close to the passenger-side door as he could get, the way he was now. "How did the meeting go with DrillTech?" he asked to banish the dangerous thought.

"They have some interesting proposals about horizontal drilling, but I want to see what the other firms have to offer before I make a decision." Linc pulled the truck into a space in the parking lot next to Cindi's but didn't say anything else until they were seated. After the waitress handed them menus and took their order for two iced teas and corned beef sandwiches, the smile Linc gave her faded as she walked away. "I'm sorry if Melissa's been giving you a hard time when she called. You should have let me know. Dealing with her isn't part of your job description." He gave a short laugh. "Though I guess if you hadn't done such a great job of picking out gifts for her, she wouldn't have gotten her hopes up. Guess that won't be part of your job anymore either. Sometimes I just don't understand women."

That makes two of us, Jonah thought. Caylee was the only woman he'd ever come close to understanding, and he still didn't know what she saw in Jack Ballinger. He couldn't imagine anyone lucky enough to date Linc throwing that away. "I didn't mind. Though I'm sorry she got so nasty about it. Can she really make things hard for you?" There was no way he believed Linc had done anything to lead Melissa on, but that wouldn't matter much if other people gave credence to her lies.

"She can say anything she wants about me." Linc paused when the waitress returned with their drinks. "People who know me won't listen to her, and I don't give much of a good goddamn about anybody else."

"But can she really hurt your business?"

Linc chuckled. "People buy my beef because of its quality, not because of what they might think about me personally. Don't lose any sleep over it—I won't be going broke any time soon. Your job is secure."

"I'm not worried about my job. I'm worried about you." As soon as he said it, Jonah could have kicked himself. Luckily the waitress showed up with their plates, giving him a chance to take a deep breath and hope his face wasn't as red as it felt.

Linc gave him a thoughtful look before taking a bite of his sandwich. Fortunately he didn't seem to have read anything into Jonah's admission other than friendly concern. "You ought to come out to the ranch one day this week," he said after a moment. "It will give you a chance to get more familiar with both sides of the operation—the cattle and the energy leases—in person. I'd be happy to drive you out there if you'd like to come."

Jonah nearly choked on his mouthful of corned beef and had to take a drink of iced tea to wash it down. Of course he'd love to visit the Broken Spoke, but if he could barely keep from giving away his attraction at a simple business lunch like this, how would he manage spending a whole a day with Linc? At least in the office they spent much of the time working separately, but unless Linc passed him off to one of his ranch hands to show him around, it would mean they'd be together the entire day. His traitorous mind formed a picture of Linc in tight-fitting jeans, the denim worn in all the right places, the snaps on his Western shirt half-undone in the heat. On horseback, where the saddle would frame his firm ass perfectly…. Jonah closed his eyes and fought off a wave of arousal. It would be a dream come true, but keeping his feelings for Linc from slipping out could be a nightmare.

"Your friends are welcome to come along if they like," Linc added when Jonah realized he hadn't given him an answer.

"That would be great," he managed to force out. "I'll ask them when I get home tonight."

"Good," Linc said with a smile. "Let's plan it for this Friday."

Jonah hoped his smile back wasn't as strained as it felt.

"SHEESH, what a day!" Jonah collapsed onto a chair at their small dining table. Wes was in the kitchen cooking something that smelled amazing involving bacon.

"That bad?" Wes answered. "I thought every day was perfect in Linc-land. What happened?"

"What didn't happen?" Jonah groaned. "And what are you making? It smells delicious."

"Hot German potato salad. Aidan's grilling some burgers and brats on that new stainless-steel monster he bought." He turned off the burner and crossed the space to the table, then turned a chair around and straddled it backward. "Now, spill. What's going on?"

"Linc's girlfriend showed up at the office today." He'd told Wes enough about Melissa that Wes nodded for him to continue. "He was in a meeting and wasn't expecting her, and she got upset at having to wait for him. When he finally wrapped up the meeting and had time for her, she blew up. She pitched a fit—with me sitting right there—and Linc wound up showing her the door."

"From what you've told me, that sounds like a good thing," Wes observed.

"For him, maybe, but not for me." Jonah frowned. "At least when he was dating her, I could tell myself he was already taken. Now I don't have that rationale anymore."

"So maybe he'll finally notice your sterling attributes."

"He's still straight," Jonah reminded him. "He knows I'm gay, but I don't want to jeopardize my job by letting him know how I feel about him. I already had a close call at lunch today."

"Jonah, he seemed like a decent guy when I met him the night of the wine walk. He doesn't seem like the type to fire you even if he did find out you have a crush on him."

It might have started out as a crush, Jonah knew, but as he'd gotten to know Linc better over the past weeks, he couldn't dismiss it that easily. Somehow he'd fallen in love with Lincoln Courtwright, but he wasn't ready to admit that to anyone, even Wes.

Before he could come up with a reply, the back door opened and Sammy and Aidan came into the kitchen. Aidan carried a platter of grilled meats and veggie burgers, and Sammy had a tray of sliced tomatoes, lettuce, red onions, avocados, and several kinds of cheese, along with a bag of fresh-baked buns. "Dinner is served," Sammy announced, setting his offerings on the counter next to the burgers and bratwurst. "Get it while it's hot."

Jonah waited until they'd finished eating before bringing up Linc's invitation. "So, my boss asked if we'd like to spend the day at the Broken Spoke on Friday. He wants to let me get familiar with the cattle and oil and gas business firsthand, but he invited all of you to come too if you're interested."

Sammy shook his head. "Can you imagine this fabulousness"—he swept a hand to indicate his mesh tank top and tropical-print jeans—"on a ranch? With nasty, smelly cows and horses and who knows what? Thank you, darling, but I'll pass."

"And I wouldn't mind seeing it, but I have to work," Aidan said.

Jonah turned a pleading glance at Wes. "I'm supposed to work Friday night, but I suppose I could see if Nate would trade with me for Saturday instead," he replied. "I wouldn't be able to go clubbing with you Saturday night, but I don't suppose you'd mind missing that. Though I don't know why you're so nervous about going on your own. You grew up on a ranch, after all."

"I grew up on a farm," Jonah answered. "Even the biggest ranches around us weren't a tenth the size of the Broken Spoke."

"Yeah, but it's not the ranch that's the problem, is it?" Wes said with a wicked grin. "It's the thought of spending the day alone with your sexy-hot boss in all his cowboy glory."

Aidan and Sammy snickered. *The problem with friends is that they know you too well*, Jonah reflected. Not that he'd give his up for the world. "So will you come with me or not?"

"As long as I can switch days," Wes agreed. "Though you'd be just fine going on your own if I can't. After all, what's the worst that could happen?"

After the day he'd just had, Jonah didn't want to tempt fate to find out.

Chapter Nine

"WES, come on! We have to get going." Jonah paced at the bottom of the stairs, anxious to get on the road. Wes had been able to switch days with a coworker so he could come along with Jonah to Linc's ranch, but since he usually worked evenings, he wasn't a morning person, and getting him moving could take some effort. "If you don't get your butt down here now, I'm going to leave without you."

"After giving me the big pleading puppy-dog eyes to trade days with Nate? Yeah, right." Wes ambled down the stairs, yawning. "I hope you made a big pot of coffee. I'll have to mainline it to get moving this early."

"Seriously? You're wearing that?" Jonah gestured at Wes's T-shirt, which proclaimed "Yes, I am from Texas. No, I am not a steer."

"I thought it was appropriate, seeing as we're going to a ranch."

Jonah shook his head. "There's a travel mug of coffee for you on the table. Put your shoes on and let's go."

"How likely am I to step on a cow patty?" Wes asked. "I'd hate to ruin my new Vans." Luckily for Jonah's self-control, Wes grinned. "I'm just winding you up, Jo. Unlike Sammy, I don't mind risking my fabulousness for the greater good." He pulled on his rainbow-hued slip-ons and grabbed the coffee mug from the table. "Let's do it."

IT took nearly three hours to reach the ranch, though negotiating his way through morning traffic in both Dallas and Fort Worth was the worst part of the drive. Wes dozed off for part of the way, giving Jonah more time than he needed to second-guess whether this was a good idea, but there was no reasonable explanation he could give Linc to back out. And he really did want to see the ranch and in particular learn a bit more about the oil- and gas-drilling procedures. He hoped they'd prove interesting enough to keep his attention from wandering to his all too fascinating boss.

Once he left Interstate 30 for the smaller state roads, Jonah nudged Wes to help navigate. "Google Maps to the rescue," Wes declared, pulling up the app on his phone and instructing Jonah when to turn, the last onto a two-lane road with a Ranch to Market designation.

"Linc said the ranch wouldn't be hard to find," Jonah said hesitantly a bit later.

"I'd guess that's it." Wes pointed to a metal arch that interrupted the miles of fencing they'd driven past.

At the top of the arch dangled a wagon wheel with a missing spoke.

Jonah turned down the well-maintained dirt road, though it was a good mile, at least, before they saw more than pastureland on either side of the drive. Finally they approached a sprawling wooden ranch house, with gabled windows quartering the roof and a wide porch stretching across the front of the building. "Not quite as fancy as the one on *Dallas*," Wes commented while Jonah parked, "but it's still pretty impressive."

By the time they got out of the truck, Linc was waiting for them on the porch. "Welcome to the Broken Spoke. Hope you didn't have any trouble finding the place."

"No problems once we got out of the metroplex," Jonah said. Linc wasn't dressed much differently than most days in the office. His jeans might be a bit more worn and faded, his boots more obviously for work than for dress, but somehow the slight differences made him all the more appealing in Jonah's eyes. Or maybe it was his attitude, Jonah realized. Linc was never much for formality, but he seemed just a bit more relaxed, his smile just a bit warmer, as if being on the ranch as opposed to the city grounded him. Jonah realized he was staring and hastily dropped his gaze. "You remember my friend Wes."

"Yes, of course." Linc offered his hand with a smile. "Like your shirt." Wes shot a smirk at Jonah before extending his hand in return. "It's fixing to be a hot one already. Come on inside and have some tea before we get started."

The inside of the house was as inviting as the outside, with smooth wooden floors and whitewashed walls, and a mix of furniture that had clearly been in the family for generations blended together with newer pieces in a warm and welcoming space. An older woman sat on one of the couches, a tray holding a sweating pitcher of iced tea and several glasses on the table in front of her.

"Jonah, Wes, this is Eloise Courtwright, my late father's wife. Eloise, this is my associate Jonah Hollis and his friend Wes—" He hesitated, and Jonah tried to remember if he'd ever told him Wes's last name.

"Paterson," Wes said, leaning forward to offer her his hand.

The woman took in his blue hair, tattooed arms, and T-shirt, and her expression tightened. "Pleased to meet you," she said stiffly, shaking Wes's hand with a moue of distaste, then dropping it as quickly as possible.

Linc frowned but didn't comment on her reaction. "Please, sit," he said. "Eloise, would you serve the tea, please?" The older woman poured four glasses and placed them around the tray, then set to adding sugar to hers, clearly not intending to initiate any conversation.

"Riding's the best way to see the property," Linc began after an awkward pause. "I can have horses saddled for both of you, if you'd like."

"I've never been on a horse," Wes said with a grin. "City boy, born and bred."

That had never occurred to Jonah, and he glanced at Wes apologetically.

"I can put you on our gentlest horse, or we can take the truck, though that would limit us to staying on the roads in some places," Linc offered.

"No, you two go on ahead. I'll just stay here and have a nice cozy visit with Eloise." Wes drained his glass of tea and poured himself another.

"Are you sure?" Jonah whispered to Wes as Linc finished his drink and stood. The whole purpose of bringing Wes along was so he wouldn't be alone with Linc, but he could hardly insist on Wes accompanying them.

"Absolutely! Go enjoy your ride. I'll be just fine here."

Jonah rose with a sigh and turned to follow Linc. As they headed out the door, he could hear Wes say to Eloise, "That's a lovely dress you're wearing. I have one almost like it myself...." He gave Jonah a wink before they walked outside.

"Do you think it's safe to leave them alone?" Jonah asked as Linc led him toward the barn he could see a little way from the house. "I apologize in advance for all the outrageous things Wes will say to her."

"I apologize for her attitude," Linc countered. "But it looks like Wes is more than able to stand up for himself." He paused when they reached the barn. "How well do you ride?"

"We didn't keep our own horses on the farm, but I had enough friends who did that I learned how," Jonah said. "As long as you don't put me on a bucking bronc, I should be okay."

Linc chuckled. "No broncs here at the moment. I think I'll put you on Honcho. He shouldn't give you any trouble." He led Jonah to a handsome roan munching placidly on some hay. "Can you saddle him yourself?"

"Sure," Jonah answered. It had been a few years since he'd ridden last, but that was one of the first things he'd learned and not something he'd forgotten.

"Tack's over there." Linc pointed to a wall of shelves holding blankets, saddles, and bridles. "Pick anything you like—Honcho's not particular."

Jonah chose what he'd need and opened Honcho's stall, careful to move slowly so he wouldn't spook the horse. "Hi there, boy," he said softly. "How's about you let me ride you today?" Honcho raised his head to look at him but didn't offer any objection, so Jonah began the process of tacking him up.

By the time he was finished, Linc was waiting for him outside the barn, standing beside a beautiful dun horse. He handed Jonah a straw Stetson. "The sun can get pretty bad out here, and there isn't a lot of shade. I think this should fit you."

Jonah set it on his head. "Thanks. I wore boots, but I didn't think about a hat." Not that he had a hat like this one with him in Dallas, but he could have at least worn a baseball cap or something to keep from getting sunstroke.

Linc put on his own hat and mounted the dun easily. Jonah swallowed against a flare of arousal at watching Linc swing a long leg over his horse's back and settle his tight ass into the saddle. Before Linc could notice the thickness under Jonah's jeans, he swung into Honcho's saddle, hiding the twinge of discomfort as it pressed against his cock. *That should get rid of my inappropriate reaction*, he thought, following Linc as he rode out of the barn's covered paddock.

"It's not that I minded my father remarrying," Linc said after they'd ridden a ways from the house. "My mother passed when I was six. He was alone for a lot of years."

"Oh, I'm so sorry," Jonah said. He tried to picture Linc as a young towheaded boy, having to deal with losing his mother at such a young age.

"She was pregnant, and there were complications," Linc said. "The baby came too soon, and the doctors couldn't save either of them. My dad took it hard. He wasn't the most demonstrative of men, but he closed up a little more after that."

Jonah's heart ached for Linc as much as for his father, but he wasn't sure what to say that wouldn't sound like an empty platitude. They rode a bit farther without speaking.

"I was already away at college when he met Eloise," Linc eventually continued. *That explains why he doesn't refer to her as his stepmother*, Jonah thought. "Whatever I think of her, she made him happy. I just wish she wasn't quite so...." Linc was clearly having trouble finding the right word to describe her.

Homophobic? Jonah thought, though he wouldn't say that to Linc. *Hidebound? Crotchety?* "Conservative?" he finally offered.

"That's one way to put it," Linc said with a laugh. "You're lucky to still have both your parents, even if it may not always seem like it." He took off his hat, ran a hand through his hair, and settled it back on his head. "Anyway, I'm supposed to be showing you the ranch, not boring you with my life story."

It wasn't anything close to his life story, Jonah thought, though he was thrilled that Linc felt comfortable enough to share even that much. There was still so much more he wanted to know, but he wouldn't pry. Linc would tell him, or not, in his own good time. "I bored you with mine," Jonah reminded him instead. "That makes us even."

LINC turned to purely business topics after that, and by the time they rode back toward the house for lunch, Jonah's head was whirling with the number of cattle the ranch ran at any given time, the amount of pasture they grazed, and the logistics of determining which to breed, which to cull, and which to sell for beef. Linc pointed out the bunkhouses where the ranch hands lived and the various barns and outbuildings used for marking the herd, breeding—both natural and artificial—and treating any injured cattle. They passed several wells as they rode, and Linc promised to tell him more about the capture and transportation of the ranch's gas and oil reserves after they ate.

Jonah couldn't help but feel a bit apprehensive about what they'd find when they returned to the ranch house. Wes wasn't malicious, but he'd obviously picked up on Eloise's reaction to his appearance and seemed ready to play it up for all it was worth.

"Well, the house is still standing and your truck is still here," Linc said as they approached, so he must have shared some of the same concern. "I'll take those as good signs."

When they rode up to the barn, a tall, wiry cowboy with a shock of blond hair was waiting to meet them. Linc introduced them after they dismounted. "Jonah, this is my foreman, Ford Slater. Ford, Jonah Hollis."

"We've talked on the phone," Ford acknowledged, shaking Jonah's hand. "Boss, that outfit that bought some of the brood cows wants to talk about picking up some more if we can spare them. As long as you're here, I thought you'd want to talk with them yourself." Linc nodded, and Ford continued, "I can take care of Cíbolo if you want to call them now."

"If you don't mind?" Linc asked Jonah. "I'd just as soon handle it right away so we have the afternoon free. Business before pleasure and all."

"Of course," Jonah said, a bit flattered that Linc considered spending the afternoon with him a pleasure rather than work. Before he could censor the thought, Linc was on his way to the house, and Ford was unbuckling Cíbolo's saddle.

"It's a pleasure to finally meet you," Ford said after Jonah set Honcho's saddle and blanket on the rail separating the barn from the paddock. "Linc hasn't brought a man here to the ranch since his father died."

Ford's meaning didn't penetrate at first, but when it did, Jonah was sure he flushed to the roots of his hair. "Oh no, it's not like that," he stammered. "It's just—he thought I should get to see the ranch. We're not—he's not—I didn't know he was—"

"Bi?" Ford finished the sentence for him. "He doesn't act on it much now, but back in college, when he was still competing in the rodeo, he had buckle bunnies of both sexes coming on to him."

Jonah vaguely remembered Linc telling him he and Ford had roomed together at A&M.

"Old man Courtwright never much minded how he sowed his wild oats, but once he was gone, Linc didn't want to offend Eloise's sensibilities, I suppose." Ford's expression made it plain what he thought of those sensibilities.

"But we aren't—it's not like that!" Jonah insisted. *Only in my wildest dreams.*

"Wouldn't matter to me any if it was."

Jonah shook his head, and Ford raised an eyebrow but let it drop, to Jonah's great relief.

"Lunch is on the table," he said, gesturing for Jonah to precede him. Jonah took a deep breath and started toward the house, wondering how he could possibly face Linc knowing what he now did.

Chapter Ten

FORD led Jonah through the back door, giving a wink to the woman in the kitchen—probably the housekeeper, Jonah thought—before they entered a large dining room. As he'd promised, the table was already set, and platters of sliced beef, coleslaw, potato salad, and rolls were set out on the snowy tablecloth. Linc must not have finished his call yet, since the room's only occupants were Wes, who flashed Jonah an unrepentant grin, and Eloise, whose dour expression seemed unchanged. Hoping that meant Wes hadn't been too outrageous while they were gone, Jonah brought Ford over to meet him.

"Wes, this is Linc's foreman, Ford Slater. Ford, this is my—" He'd normally introduce Wes as his roommate, but given Eloise's attitude, he amended that. "—my friend Wes Paterson."

"We live together," Wes announced sunnily, dashing Jonah's hopes that he'd toned things down.

Ford took Wes's hand with a smile. "Well, aren't you a purty little thing," he drawled.

Wes grinned in return. "Well, hello to you too, tall, blond, and handsome."

Fortunately Linc returned at that moment, or Jonah was afraid Eloise might have popped a blood vessel.

"I agreed to sell him another fifty head," he told Ford, though the look that passed between them seemed to be about more than just cattle. "You might as well stay for lunch. I can fill you in on the details before we ride out again."

"Suits me," Ford agreed. "I'll take Marcela's cooking over the chuck wagon any day."

When they were seated around the table and everyone had served themselves, Jonah had to agree the food was delicious. The beef brisket was flavorful without being dry, the crisply charred ends adding a richer flavor.

"Did you smoke this yourself?" Wes asked.

"Got a smoker out back I put in a few years back," Linc confirmed.

Wes took another bite and hummed with pleasure.

"Linc does love his barbecue," Ford added, though his attention was on Wes.

"We have *got* to get a smoker," Wes told Jonah. "See how the color goes all the way through the meat? It's the only way to get that flavor."

"I thought the ribs you made with the dry rub last week were pretty amazing," Jonah said.

"Yeah, but I had to slow-roast them in the oven and age them for days before Aidan grilled them. I could get the same results with a smoker in a day."

"You a chef?" Ford asked, taking another helping of brisket.

"Just a foodie for now, but someday," Wes said.

"In the meantime, he mixes a fine cocktail," Linc added. "So how did you two amuse yourselves while I was showing Jonah around?"

Jonah wasn't sure he wanted to hear the answer to that question, but Wes grinned.

"Eloise told me about the Courtwright family history. She's traced the family tree back to medieval England. She's got their coat of arms and everything."

"The name originally defined an occupation, meaning a maker of carts and wheels." It was the most Jonah had heard Eloise volunteer all day, and her voice was almost warm. "Which makes the name 'Broken Spoke' for the ranch quite appropriate. Though to have been awarded a coat of arms, of course, the family rose to the level of nobility well before some of them migrated to America. There were Courtwrights in the colonies as early as the 1600s."

"I've got to do more research into my genealogy." The gleam in Wes's eyes was one Jonah had learned to distrust. "I'm sure there are several queens in my family tree."

Ford bit off what sounded suspiciously like a chuckle, and Jonah concentrated on finishing the food on his plate. This meal couldn't be over fast enough.

"I had lunch at the country club yesterday, and Katherine Eldridge told me that she saw Melissa having dinner with John Maxwell," Eloise said after a few moments of silence. "According to her, they looked quite... comfortable together."

"Didn't take her long to land on her feet," Ford muttered. "And with him, of all people."

Linc shot him a warning glance but said nothing.

"You'd better act fast if you hope to win her back, Lincoln. There's a rumor that he's already asked her to be his guest at the Cattle Baron's Ball next month."

Jonah didn't know what the Cattle Baron's Ball was, but it sounded important, if Eloise's tone was any indication.

"I'm happy for her," Linc said dryly.

"Such a lovely young woman," Eloise continued, as if Linc hadn't spoken. "The two of you are perfect together. I'm sure if you made an effort, this misunderstanding between you could be cleared up."

Linc pushed away his plate and stood. "Eloise, I appreciate your concern, but my personal life is none of your business. Please thank Marcela for lunch. Ford, I need to talk to you about the terms of the breeder sale. Jonah, don't let me rush you from finishing your meal. You can join us whenever you're ready." Jonah had never heard his voice sound so curt. Without waiting for Ford, he stalked out of the dining room.

Ford dropped his napkin on his plate and rose. "When the boss says jump.... Nice to meet you both," he said, flashing a smile at Jonah and Wes before following Linc out.

There was still some food left on Jonah's plate, but he couldn't force himself to finish it. After moving it around with his fork for a few minutes in awkward silence, he gave up and pushed his chair away from the table. He wasn't sure it was safe to leave Wes alone again with Eloise, but he couldn't sit there with her either. It was a good thing she hadn't made the same assumption Ford had, or she'd be tossing him and Wes out the door as fast as she could. Giving Wes a glance he hoped would be understood as a plea not to make things any worse, he headed back for the barn.

JONAH had almost reached the paddock when he heard Linc's and Ford's voices coming from inside the barn. He was about to join them when he thought he caught Melissa's name, stopping him in his tracks. Eloise's words at lunch—*I'm sure if you made an effort, this misunderstanding between you could be cleared up*—came back to him, and he wondered whether Linc might be regretting having broken things off with Melissa so abruptly, especially if she was already seeing someone else. Linc's response had been more short-tempered than Jonah had ever seen him, and while that might have been due to Eloise's interference, it might also be because he was regretting his impulsive reaction to Melissa's ultimatum. Jonah walked quietly to the side of the barn, careful to stay out of sight of anyone inside.

"—heard tell she's been bad-mouthing you to anyone who'll listen," he heard Ford say.

"She can say anything she likes. No one who matters will believe her."

"If she'd taken up with anyone but Big John Maxwell, it wouldn't be so bad," Ford complained. "It's like she deliberately hooked up with the one person guaranteed to rile you."

"I wouldn't have a problem with John if he'd keep his overspray out of my fields," Linc said. "I can't graze any cattle in the pastures that border his land or I'll risk losing our organic certification, but he's too bullheaded to listen to reason. He and Melissa ought to get along just fine."

"Marcela told me pretty much the same thing Eloise said—that he's already asked her to the Cattle Baron's Ball. She'll be flaunting him in your face all night."

"Not if I'm not there," Linc retorted. "Hell, I'd just as soon miss that whole high-society rigmarole, anyway. They get the money whether I go or not, and that will leave two more seats at the table for someone else from the ranch to attend."

"And Melissa will spend the whole time claiming you're too heartbroken to face her." Ford snorted. "You can't give her that satisfaction. Besides, I don't want to spend the night having to listen to Eloise bitching if you don't show up."

"She would, too." Linc sighed.

"And you can't show up without a date either. Melissa would make even more hay out of that than if you didn't show up at all," Ford insisted.

"But I don't have a date."

"Find one."

"Easy for you to say. I'll think about it, okay? That's the best I can promise at the moment."

"Fair enough," Ford said. "So what do you want to do about the brood cows?"

At least it didn't sound like Linc was missing Melissa any, Jonah thought with relief. Though he didn't want to think about Linc dating anyone, he hoped whoever he found would be better for him than Melissa. Since the personal discussion seemed to be over, he squared his shoulders and entered the barn as if he'd just walked from the house. Linc glanced up and nodded at him, giving no indication he suspected Jonah had overheard the earlier conversation.

"Pick out the ones you think we can spare and send the information to Jonah," Linc said to Ford, taking up Cíbolo's tack and then heading toward the paddock. "We'll invoice Jackson when we're back in the office."

While Jonah resaddled Honcho, taking a little longer since he didn't want to risk hurting or spooking one of Linc's horses, Linc and Ford talked through getting the cattle ready to deliver.

"Want to join us?" Linc asked Ford when Jonah mounted up.

"Nah, I don't need to hang around the rigs until the next time we're ready to transport. I'll get started on picking out the new batch of cows. Y'all have a good ride. See you soon, Jonah."

Jonah couldn't imagine when Ford expected to see him again unless Linc invited him back to the ranch someday, since the foreman had never come into the office. But he nodded and waved, even though he was a bit relieved Ford wouldn't be accompanying them.

"Sorry you had to overhear that. You seem to get caught in the middle of all my uncomfortable conversations lately," Linc said as he led them in a different direction than they'd ridden that morning.

For a panicked instant, Jonah thought Linc knew he'd been eavesdropping after all. Then he realized Linc must be referring to Eloise's comments at lunch. "She just wants what's best for you, I'm sure," he said finally. *Even though that definitely isn't getting you back together with Melissa.*

"She wants me to marry well—by her definition of that phrase, not mine—and ensure the next generation to carry on the Courtwright name." Linc scowled. "Ah hell, I don't want to go over all that again. Just sorry she had to bring it up in front of you."

"I didn't know you used to be part of the rodeo circuit," Jonah said, scrambling for a way to change the subject and wipe the gloomy frown from Linc's face.

"Who told you about that?" Linc asked, his expression changing to one of surprise. "It was way before your time."

"Ford mentioned it." Jonah stopped short, remembering what else Ford had mentioned. *I will not think about Linc being bi. I will not!* "What—" He swallowed hard to hide the tremor in his voice. "What events did you compete in?"

"Saddle bronc riding and calf roping—skills I could use here on the ranch."

No wonder he looks so natural sitting Cíbolo, Jonah thought. "I wish I'd had a chance to see you compete."

"That was back in my wild college days. Ford and I made quite a pair in College Station before my dad got sick." That brought a frown back to Linc's face, and Jonah was trying to think of some other topic he could bring up when Linc seemed to shake off his momentary melancholy. "There's one of the wells up ahead."

Jonah pushed the image of Linc's strong thighs wrapped around a wildly bucking horse from his mind and prepared to focus on the mechanics of oil and gas drilling.

Chapter Eleven

"C'MON, Jonah, enough work for the morning. Let's rustle up some grub," Linc said, coming out of his inner office to lean over Jonah's desk in the way that always sent Jonah's pulse racing.

"That would be great," Jonah replied. In the weeks since his visit to the Broken Spoke, he and Linc had eaten lunch together every day Linc was in the office. Linc had decreed that they couldn't talk about work during meals, so Jonah had told Linc more about his parents and growing up on the family farm, and Linc had shared stories from his days riding in the rodeo circuit. Those hours had become the highlight of Jonah's week.

"What's that you're reading?" Linc asked before Jonah could turn off his monitor.

Jonah could feel himself flush, though there was no reason for him to be embarrassed. It wasn't like he was looking at porn or even reading personal e-mails on business time. "Just an article about slim-hole and coiled-tube drilling."

"Just some light reading for relaxation, huh?" Linc shook his head. "You are a treasure, that's for sure. I struck a bonanza when I hired you."

This time Jonah was sure he blushed. "Everything you showed me at the ranch was so interesting, about the different drilling methods and how the gas is converted to a liquid for storage and transport. I've been trying to educate myself about it."

"And I appreciate it, but no talking—"

"—business during lunch," Jonah finished with him, making Linc laugh.

"Right, so get your butt out of that chair and let's go. There's a new Mexican restaurant I want us to try." Linc waited for Jonah to leave the office before him, still smiling as he locked up and drove the short distance down Main Street.

As soon as they walked into Wild Salsa, the aromas of sizzling meat, peppers, and onions tantalized Jonah's senses. "Wes would love this place," he commented, taking in the colorful *Día de los Muertos*-themed decor.

"And they use locally sourced ingredients, from what I saw on their website," Linc added.

Once they were seated and had placed their orders—Jonah chose the carnitas tamales, while Linc opted for arrachera steak tacos—Linc leaned forward and rested his forearms on the table, bringing him close enough for Jonah to detect a hint of his crisp cologne. Jonah's mouth suddenly felt dry, and he licked his lips before taking a drink of the ice water a server had just refilled.

"Jonah, I'd like to ask you something," Linc said. "It's not related to work, so don't feel you're obligated in any way…." He fell uncharacteristically silent.

Jonah couldn't imagine anything Linc might ask him that he wouldn't agree to, but he waited for Linc to continue.

"I'd like you to come to the Cattle Baron's Ball with me next month."

Whatever he'd thought Linc might ask him, it surely wasn't that. "I—I'm not sure what that is," he admitted. "I remember Eloise mentioned it when we were at the ranch…." *Because Melissa was going to be there with someone else.*

"It's a fund-raising event for the American Cancer Society," Linc explained. "It's an annual event that started back in 1974, and since then it's raised nearly sixty million dollars for local cancer research." He paused while their waitress set their plates in front of them, asked whether they wanted anything else, and topped off their drinks before stepping away. "It's something I've supported ever since my dad passed from pancreatic cancer."

Jonah couldn't help but remember the conversation he'd overheard between Linc and Ford, that same day on the ranch.

"*Melissa will spend the whole time claiming you're too heartbroken to face her*," Ford had argued.

"*I don't have a date*," Linc had objected.

To which Ford had answered, "*Find one.*"

He couldn't believe Linc hadn't been able to find anyone else to accompany him, but then he didn't know much about how events like this worked. If it was anything like prom back in high school, maybe people had their dates set up months in advance, and anyone

Linc might have thought to ask was already committed to going with someone else. Jonah didn't fool himself that he was anything but a last-minute desperation choice. Why else would Linc have waited weeks after Ford pointed out he needed a date to ask him?

He hadn't gone to his prom. He'd have no idea how to behave at a charity ball. He couldn't do this.

Jonah shook his head. "I wouldn't fit in at a society event like that." *I'd be afraid I'd do something to embarrass you*, he thought, though he couldn't admit that out loud. "Besides, shouldn't your date be… a woman?"

"This is the twenty-first century, Jonah," Linc countered. "Same-sex couples have the right to get married, even in the great state of Texas. All I'm asking is for you to come to a dance with me."

"It's not a dance, it's a ball." *And I'm sure as heck no Cinderella.* He had to laugh. "I can't believe I'm saying this, but I wouldn't even have the right clothes to wear."

"Hell, that's no problem," Linc said. "This is a boots-and-blue-jeans kind of affair. For a lot of years, it was held out at actual ranches. They had some problems with bad weather recently, so they've taken to holding it at indoor sites to be safe. This year it's going to be at Gilley's, right outside of downtown. And if you really need to buy some new clothes, you've got the company card. Just put whatever you need on there."

Linc made it all sound so easy, but Jonah was torn. He couldn't imagine himself at a fancy society event, but the chance to spend a night with Linc—maybe even in his arms, dancing—was too tempting to resist, even if the only reason Linc was asking him was so he wouldn't look bad in front of Melissa.

He took a deep breath. "Okay," he said. "I'll go with you."

"I CAN'T believe I said yes," Jonah moaned to Wes hours later. It had sounded reasonable while Linc was persuading him, but he'd second-guessed himself all afternoon, imagining all the ways things could go horribly wrong. "I'm going to tell him tomorrow morning that I changed my mind."

"Why on earth would you do that?" Wes stopped stirring the peanut sauce for the chicken satay skewers he'd given Aidan to grill and stared at Jonah. "The man you've been drooling over since you started to work for him finally asks you out for more than lunch, and you're going to say no? What is wrong with you?"

"Because he isn't asking me out—not like that, anyway. He has to have someone with him because Melissa is going to be there with someone else. He just doesn't want it to look like he's pining for her or anything."

"You don't know that."

"Actually, yeah, I do." No matter how embarrassing it was, Wes deserved to know the truth. "I heard him and Ford talking that day at the ranch."

Wes smiled for a moment. "My tall, blond cowboy." His expression sobered as he looked back at Jonah. "You know eavesdroppers never hear anything good."

"That doesn't mean it isn't true. Melissa's going to be there with another rancher, and if Linc doesn't go or shows up alone, she's going to make it seem like he's still broken up over her. I'll just be pretending to be his date."

"Did Linc tell you that when he asked you to go?"

"No, but why else would he ask me? Even if he used to date men back in college"—though the impression he'd gotten from Ford was more like one-time hookups—"he hasn't asked me to anything but business meals. I can't let myself imagine it's anything more than that." He wouldn't admit it to anyone other than Wes, but he had to be honest. "I can't risk falling in love with him." *So much for honesty*, he thought. *It's already too late for that.*

"The answer to that is to make him fall in love with you," Wes said, wiping his hands on the towel tucked into his belt before coming around the table to hug Jonah. "Don't be so down on yourself. If he could put up with dating someone as shallow as Melissa, you just have to show him what he's been missing."

As if it's that easy, Jonah thought. "I'm sure she had some redeeming qualities."

"Yeah, the size of her tits," Wes retorted.

"And how am I supposed to compete with that?"

"You don't have to. Your ass is better than hers. And if Linc *is* bi, I guarantee you he's noticed."

"Noticed what?" Aidan asked, coming inside with the platter of satay kabobs.

"Jonah's ass," Wes answered, moving the peanut sauce and rice with chickpeas onto the table.

"And such a *fiiine* ass it is too," Sammy agreed as he joined the others in the kitchen. "Why are we talking about Jonah's ass?"

"Because his boss asked him to the Cattle Baron's Ball."

Before Wes could add anything more, Sammy squealed in delight. "Oh, you lucky, lucky gay boy! The Cattle Baron's Ball is *the* social event of the season in Dallas."

"It doesn't matter if it's the social event of the country," Jonah said, "because I'm not going."

"That is just plain foolishness. You have to represent for all the rest of us," Sammy insisted.

"Can you imagine me at a fancy charity event?"

"I can," Aidan answered. "What's the big deal? They're just people like everyone else."

"People with a lot more money than I'll ever have."

"What difference does that make?" Sammy demanded. "Besides, you'll be looking so edible, they'll all wish they were you."

"Linc said it was just a boots-and-blue-jeans affair," Jonah said uncertainly.

"There are boots, and then there are boots, if you know what I mean. You surely can't show up in the jeans and ropers you wore to visit his ranch."

Since that was exactly what Jonah had planned, it only reinforced his certainty that he needed to tell Linc he couldn't go. His dismay must have shown on his face, because Sammy smiled.

"Never you mind, baby. I'll take you shopping and get you fixed up right. Leave it to me, and you will be the beau of the ball."

He knew Sammy meant to be reassuring, but the idea left Jonah terrified.

Chapter Twelve

BY morning, despite his friends' best efforts to convince him otherwise, Jonah had decided he was going to tell Linc he couldn't do it. He'd spent hours online after dinner looking at the Cattle Baron's Ball website, especially the photo galleries from previous years. It might be a boots-and-blue-jeans affair for the men, though Sammy was definitely right that there were boots, and then there were *boots*. But it was the way the women dressed—designer gowns, elegant hairstyles, jewelry that made the tennis bracelet he'd ordered for Melissa look like a Girl Scout craft project—that convinced him how out of place he'd be. How could it possibly help Linc's status in society to go from having someone like Melissa on his arm to escorting someone like him?

No matter how often he might have daydreamed himself into Melissa's place with Linc, Jonah had known that's all it could ever be—dreams. To have the chance to act out those dreams, knowing it was all a pretense designed to help Linc save face, would be exquisite torture. How could he go back to only dealing with Linc as his boss when the charade was over? Better to leave it a beautiful, impossible fantasy.

On the drive to the office, he worked himself up to face Linc and back out as gracefully as he could. Hopefully Linc wouldn't be too angry, and the sooner he did it, the more time Linc would have to find someone else to invite to the event.

When he got to the building, Linc's truck wasn't in the garage. *So I'll have to wait a little longer to tell him*, Jonah scolded himself when his stomach sank. It was disappointing that he wouldn't be able to get it off his chest right away, but Linc was a morning person. He'd be in soon.

Except he wasn't. Jonah did his best to focus on the e-mails filling his in-box, but he couldn't keep from watching the time as it crept forward on his monitor. It was after ten o'clock before the outer door finally opened and Linc walked into the office.

"You're late," Jonah snapped reflexively, then slapped his hand over his mouth when he realized he'd said it out loud. Fortunately for his continued employment, Linc laughed, and just for a moment Jonah forgot his misgivings and let himself smile back.

"You can dock my paycheck, boss," Linc said. "I had to run an errand this morning." He set a small package onto Jonah's desk. "It's something to thank you for accepting my invitation at the last minute like this. I know you're a little worried about fitting in.

though you have absolutely no reason to be, and I want to let you know how much I appreciate it."

For a moment Jonah could only stare at the gift-wrapped box, stunned. He opened his mouth, though he wasn't at all sure what he was going to say, but no words came out.

"Go on, open it," Linc urged.

Jonah reached for the package tentatively, so intent on keeping his hands from shaking that he fumbled the box but managed to grab it before it fell back onto the desk. He untaped the paper carefully, making Linc roll his eyes, and opened the lid to reveal a sporty wristwatch.

"I noticed you didn't wear a watch, so I hope it's something you can use. Though if you don't like the style, or just don't like watches, you can always exchange it for something else."

"I—no—it's great." Jonah took the watch from the case and slid it onto his wrist. The black stainless-steel band fit perfectly. "You didn't have to do this."

"And you didn't have to agree to come to the Cattle Baron's Ball with me, but I'm glad you did."

And how the heck can I tell him I'm not going after this? Jonah conceded defeat. He'd just have to man up and worry about dealing with the aftermath later. "Thank you. I guess under the circumstances, I'll let you off with a warning this time, but don't let it happen again."

Linc broke into a grin, but his expression soon turned more serious. "There's something else I'd forgotten about until Eloise reminded me. There's a party for donors coming up next week at the home of one of the organizers. If you don't have plans for Wednesday night, I'd like you to come with me."

Eloise must have let Linc know because Melissa would be there. Well, it was too late for Jonah to back out now. "I have class that night, but it won't hurt to skip it just once, so sure. I can talk to the professor on Monday to get any work I might miss."

Linc cleared his throat. "The party's actually, ah, a little more formal than the ball itself."

A nervous twisting started in the pit of Jonah's stomach. "How much more formal?"

"Not black-tie formal," Linc assured him. "A suit and tie will be fine."

Jonah tried to keep his dismay from showing on his face. The last time he'd worn a suit was when he graduated from high school. It was probably still hanging in the closet of his bedroom back home. He hadn't bothered bringing it with him to Dallas because he was pretty sure it wouldn't fit anymore. He still weighed close to the same as he did back then, but between loading trucks at work before he left Oktaha and just maturing in general, his proportions had changed. As much as he dreaded the prospect, he foresaw a shopping trip with Sammy in his immediate future. "I'm sure I can find something appropriate to wear."

"Don't forget you can use the corporate credit card if you need to," Linc offered.

He didn't have any intention of taking Linc up on that, but Jonah nodded.

"So, do you have any plans for this weekend?" Linc asked. "I thought maybe I could take you out for dinner at a place you might like in Fort Worth."

There was only one thing that could make Jonah turn down the chance to spend more time with Linc. "I can't this weekend—I'm going back to Oktaha. My best friend, Caylee's, birthday is coming up, and I always take her out to the nicest restaurant in town to celebrate. And I haven't been back since Christmas, so it will be good to see my folks too." Even if they still hadn't come to terms with his being gay.

"I'm sure it will," Linc said, and Jonah tried to convince himself he didn't look disappointed. "Well then, I'd better get to work. I have a couple of hours to make up for."

SAMMY'S reaction, when Jonah told him about the donors' party Linc also expected him to attend, almost made Jonah reconsider backing out of the whole mess. "You mean the Underwriters' Party? Only the really big donors get invited to that. Your boss must be dropping some serious bank."

"He said something about having a table," Jonah said, remembering the overheard conversation between Linc and Ford. "It sounded like other people from the ranch will be coming too."

"Oo-ooh, child, those packages start at $25,000 and go up from there. You're gonna be flying with the big boys."

Twenty-five thousand? Jonah couldn't imagine being able to spend that kind of money. Still, Linc was donating it to charity, not spending it on himself. "Which is why I need you to help me get the right clothes to wear. I don't want to embarrass Linc by not dressing right."

"Don't you worry your pretty little head. Leave it all to your fairy godfather Sammy."

Their first stop was at Boot Scootin', a local western-wear store. Sammy guided Jonah past the racks of Wranglers and Levi's to brands he'd never heard of—and when he looked at the price tags, he understood why. Still, he was relieved that Sammy eschewed any kind of embellishments, selecting several pairs of simply cut jeans for him to try on.

"See now, that's what I mean," Sammy declared, eying the contours of a pair of jeans Jonah thought were too tight but Sammy insisted fit him perfectly. "With a bubble butt like yours, you don't need any extra bling. Put a crease in those, and you will be stylin'. Now let's find you some boots."

While he could deal—barely—with a pair of jeans costing almost a hundred dollars, Jonah drew the line at the exotic boots Sammy tried to steer him toward.

"Look at the stitching on these lovelies," he cooed over a pair of caiman boots with hand-tooled embroidery.

Jonah blenched when he tipped the boot over to check the price on the bottom. At almost a thousand dollars, he was surprised the store would risk marring the sole with a price sticker. "No way am I spending a month's rent on a pair of boots, Sammy. I'm sure there are some Justins here somewhere that I can afford."

"I thought the boss man was picking up the tab," Sammy said with a bit of a pout.

Jonah touched the watch on his other wrist. "I'm not making him pay to dress me up like a Ken doll. I can't justify more than a few hundred dollars for boots, even if I can wear them later to work on the farm or to the office over the winter."

Sammy frowned, but Jonah refused to look at anything with a price tag over three hundred dollars. Eventually they were able to compromise on a pair of boots that were stylish enough for Sammy and affordable enough for Jonah to stomach.

By that time Jonah was more than ready to head home, but Sammy was indefatigable. "That was the easy part. Now we need to get you primped to mingle with the high rollers."

"Easy? Y'call that easy?" Wes or Aidan would have laughed, but Sammy either missed the reference or chose to ignore it, herding Jonah up the street to Urban Vintage.

Jonah's previous experience with buying a suit was shopping with his mom at the JCPenney in Muskogee. Unfortunately Sammy was not going to let him flip through a few coats on a rack and decide between navy and black. As soon as the sales associate heard what Jonah needed an outfit for, he ushered them to a curtained-off area at the rear of the store, where suit after suit was brought out for consideration.

"Basic black," Sammy decreed, "with a slim cut to show off the boy's killer bod." After finally narrowing the selection to three, he pointed Jonah toward the dressing room. "Here, I'll hold your wallet while you try them on."

Jonah knew he was in trouble when he got into the dressing room and found none of the garments had price tags. He couldn't help feeling a bit like one of the dolls Caylee used to play with as he paraded out each style for Sammy's evaluation. They finally agreed on a single-breasted black jacket with slim-cut slacks in a lightweight wool-silk blend. The sales clerk brought in several shirts to pair with it, and Sammy insisted he buy at least two. "You can wear the lilac shirt to the party and the white one with the jeans to the ball." There were also ties to consider, and Sammy had the salesman bring in shoes in Jonah's size to be sure the pant hems hung at just the right length. Jonah considered himself lucky

Sammy didn't insist on having him model underwear and socks to go with the ensemble.

Once the sales clerk had marked the suit for the adjustments needed to fit it to Sammy's satisfaction, Jonah was finally allowed to change back into his own clothes. When he got to the register, Sammy pushed a credit card slip in front of him. "I had them go ahead and ring everything up. Here, sign this."

The total made Jonah boggle. "Are you sure we can't just go somewhere and rent something for the night?"

Sammy glowered. "Do you want to look like someone your boss rented for the night?"

That was almost too close to the truth for Jonah, though he couldn't admit it to Sammy. He shook his head.

"I didn't think so. I had them ring this up on his credit card, and believe me, he's getting a bargain."

Jonah wasn't sure about that, but at least he wouldn't embarrass Linc by what he wore. He took a deep breath and scrawled his signature.

Chapter Thirteen

THE diner was small but clean and bright, with smells of bacon and coffee wafting out as soon as he opened the door. A few faces glanced up from various booths as Jonah entered, and he nodded in acknowledgment as he took a seat at the Formica-topped counter. Living in a small town could be a blessing or a curse; he was at least acquainted with everyone there, and it would be common knowledge by nightfall that he was back. *It's only for the weekend*, he reminded himself, pulling a plastic-covered menu from where it stood wedged between a bottle of ketchup and a sugar dispenser. He opened it even though he knew most of it by heart and was perusing the lunch offerings when a pair of arms encircled him from behind.

"Hey there, stranger. Come here often?"

He spun the stool around and broke into a grin, hugging Caylee back. "You have got to work on your pickup lines if that's the best you can manage."

"I don't have to work on picking you up. You're a sure thing." Caylee dropped onto the stool next to his with a sigh. "I must be getting old. It's hardly noon, and I'm already ready for a nap."

"You don't look a day over twenty-four," Jonah assured her. "And you'll be beautiful when you're ninety." Which was true, even if Jonah privately thought Caylee did look a little run-down. Her black hair, pulled back from her temples and caught into a clip at the top of her head, still fell in glossy curls past her shoulders, but her complexion looked paler than he remembered, and she had dark smudges under her eyes.

"I'm still twenty-three for twelve more hours, thank you very much," Caylee said, poking him. "Besides, flattery will get you nowhere. I'll always have five months on you, old man."

"God, I've missed you, Cay." Jonah leaned forward and pulled her into another hug. "I forget how much until I see you again."

"Then you just have to come back more often, Jo-Jo."

From the time they were little, no one but Caylee could get away with calling him that. He smiled but shook his head. "It wouldn't change anything. You know that."

"Have you been home to see them yet?

And that said it all about his relationship with his parents, Jonah thought, that his first stop in Oktaha was to visit Caylee rather than go home. "I had to see my best girl first. After all, I have to be sure you haven't made dinner plans for tonight with anyone but me."

"It's a permanent date," Caylee assured him. The bell on the door to the diner chimed, and Caylee pushed to her feet. "I'd better get back to work. Did you want to order something?"

Before Jonah could answer, a heavy hand fell on his shoulder. "Well, look who's back in town. Your boyfriend kick you out, Hollis?"

Jonah bit back a sigh and shrugged Jack Ballinger's hand away. "I came back to wish Caylee a happy birthday."

"Next time, send her a card." Jack turned to Caylee, and once again Jonah wondered what she saw in him. He supposed Jack was handsome enough, though his expression always seemed to be contorted into a sneer. Or maybe that was just when he looked at Jonah. "I thought we'd go see a movie or something tonight, babe."

"I already have plans with Jonah," Caylee said. "Maybe we can go tomorrow night instead."

"You're not standing me up for this queer, are you?" Jack turned to Jonah, and any warmth in his face while he'd looked at Caylee hardened to disgust. "I thought I told you I didn't want my girl hanging around with a fag like you."

Which was one of the reasons Jonah had left for Dallas, though he'd never told Caylee that. He hadn't wanted to disillusion her, but it seemed Jack had just managed to do that all on his own.

"What did you call him?" Caylee demanded, her eyes flashing with anger.

"C'mon, babe, everyone knows he's a queer. Why do you want to waste your time with him?" He smiled and tried to put his arm around her, but Caylee wasn't having it.

"Because he's my friend!" Caylee pushed Jack away with both hands. "Because he's a decent human being who's never hurt a soul, unlike you, Jackson Ballinger. How could you say something so hurtful?"

"Whoa, you're dating me, remember? And I don't want people calling my girl a fag hag."

"Then you'd better find yourself another 'girl,' because I don't want people to think I'd date a homophobic bigot like you!" Caylee pointed toward the door. "Now, unless you plan to order something, get out of here. I have customers to serve."

Jack flushed with anger and glanced around the diner as if looking for support, but most of the people who had been avidly watching the argument dropped their attention back to their plates.

One of a pair of older women sitting in the corner booth gave Caylee a smile. "Good for you, sweetheart," she called. "You may think you can teach jerks like him, but they never learn any better."

"Fine. If you'd rather spend time with this fruit, you're welcome to him." Jack glared at Jonah and stalked out of the diner. The women in the corner applauded as he left.

Caylee managed a tight smile, but it looked to Jonah like she was fighting back tears.

"I'm so sorry, Caylee," he murmured, standing to pull her into his arms. "I'd never have come back if I thought it would lead to this."

Caylee hugged him back, then blinked and shook her head. "This is *not* your fault, so don't go blaming yourself. Anyway, I'd rather know now what he's really like than for it to have gone any further." She stepped back and took a breath. "Okay, people, show's over. Jonah, can I take your order?"

AFTER eating lunch and making arrangements to pick Caylee up at her apartment at six thirty, Jonah drove from the diner down the county road to his parents' farm. He passed his father's tractor in one of fields and beeped his horn. His father raised an arm in acknowledgment but didn't stop mowing.

The two-story clapboard farmhouse seemed smaller than he remembered it, or maybe it was just in comparison to the sprawling ranch house at the Broken Spoke. He parked the truck alongside his father's newer model Ford, picked up his duffel from the seat beside him, and went inside.

He found his mother in the kitchen, canning tomatoes. Jonah couldn't remember ever seeing his mother just sitting down with her feet up. She'd laughed at him once when he'd suggested it. "*There's always chores to be done,*" she'd said, whether it was cleaning the house or doing the laundry or tending the garden or cooking meals.

"Jonah!" She turned from the stove to give him a hug. "It's good to see you."

"It's good to see you too, Mom." He remembered Linc's comment that he was lucky to still have his parents and hugged her a little longer. "Lots of tomatoes this year?"

"With all the rain, we had a bumper crop." She lifted a rack of mason jars from the canner and set them on the counter to cool. "I hope you're taking Caylee somewhere nice for dinner tonight. Now that she's broken up with Jack Ballinger, you've got another chance with her."

He shouldn't be surprised that she'd already heard about it—someone had probably called her from the diner as soon as he'd left. "Since you know about the breakup, I'm sure you also know the reason Caylee broke up with him. I love Caylee like a sister, Mom, but it's never going to be anything more than that, because I'm gay." The last three words came out in a harsher tone than he should use with his mother, but they'd had this conversation so many times before.

"If you just tried a little harder, I'm sure you could be happy with her. She's such a lovely girl. She'd help you get past this sinfulness." Her face tightened, and she shook her head. "How could you possibly find another man more attractive than Caylee?"

He'd never once lusted after Caylee, not the way he'd fantasized about Linc, but his mother would never understand that. He thought about telling her he was going to the Cattle Baron's Ball with Linc but decided it would only make things worse. If it were a real relationship, he'd tell her, even if she'd never accept it, but there was no sense getting her worked up about a charade that would end once the charity event was over.

"This isn't something I can change or you can pray away, Mom. It's who I am, and I wish you could believe that." He picked up his duffel. "I'm going to shower and get dressed for dinner." His mother's sorrowful gaze followed him up the stairs.

THE only other restaurant in Oktaha besides the diner had closed since Jonah moved to Dallas. After doing some quick research on his phone—the farm didn't have Internet access—Jonah found a restaurant in Muskogee called Miss Addie's that was located in a turn-of-the-century soda fountain. He and Caylee spent the drive up US 69 flipping through radio stations and avoiding the elephant in the cab with them, but once they reached the restaurant and placed their orders for glazed pork tenderloin and potato-crusted salmon, Jonah reached across the table and took Caylee's hand.

"I'm sorry about what happened at the diner. I can't say I'm sorry you're not dating Jack anymore, because you deserve someone so much better than him, but I'm sorry it happened the way it did."

"I never saw that side of him when you weren't around," Caylee said. "I guess you must bring out the worst in him. But I meant it when I said I'd rather know now than to have wound up married to him before I found out the truth."

"Was it that serious?" That made Jonah feel even worse, except that the idea of Caylee married to a prick like Jack was unthinkable.

"It could have been, maybe. I'm considering it a lucky escape." Caylee squeezed his hand. "But enough about my love life. I want to hear about yours." Despite the low lighting in the restaurant, Caylee must have seen him redden, because she gave a crow of laughter. "You met somebody! C'mon, spill it. Who is he?"

"It's not what you think. My boss, Mr. Courtwright—Linc—I told you about him, right?" Caylee nodded. "He's asked me as his guest to the Cattle Baron's Ball."

"A ball?" Caylee grinned. "Sounds romantic."

If only. "It's a charity event. It's a long story, but he broke things off with the woman he was dating, and he doesn't want it to look like he hasn't gotten over her by showing up alone. I'm just going to help him out. As a friend."

"Friends." She gave him her best *don't bullshit me* look. "And that's why you're blushing. Tell the truth, Jonah."

"It is the truth!" She frowned, and Jonah sighed. He'd never been able to fool Caylee. "For him, anyway.

As much as I might wish otherwise, I really am just doing him a favor. He's a fantastic guy, and he doesn't deserve Melissa making him look bad."

"Why are you so sure he doesn't feel the same way you do?" Caylee asked.

"Are you kidding? He's a millionaire with a ranch that's been in his family for six generations. I'm a farm boy from the middle of nowhere Oklahoma who never even finished college. What could he possibly see in me?"

"He'd see a kind, loving, and loyal person. There's a reason Jack doesn't like you that has nothing to do with your being gay, Jo-Jo. All through school, you're the only person who'd never back down from him when he got to acting uppity about being a Ballinger. And you always stand up for your friends. Remember when Cody Hancock fell on the playground and broke his arm? You stayed right next to him until the paramedics got there, and you wouldn't let anyone make fun of him for crying."

"That didn't stop him from calling me a 'goddamn homo' when I came out."

"I didn't say the fall knocked any sense into him." Caylee let go of his hand and stroked his cheek. "All I'm saying is, don't be so quick to decide that all your boss wants is friendship. At least be open to the possibility it could be more."

"I think I'm in love with him, Cay," Jonah admitted softly. "I don't want to fool myself into thinking he feels the same."

"Just don't convince yourself it's impossible either." Caylee grinned. "After all, you are kind of cute too—if you like pretty twinks. I might have dated you myself if only you liked girlie parts."

Jonah had to laugh. "If you think I'm a twink, someday you have got to meet Sammy." Their dinners arrived, and before long they were both laughing as he told her about the shopping expedition.

Chapter Fourteen

JONAH hadn't really expected to see Linc in the office on Monday, but he still felt a little disappointed when he didn't come in. After Caylee's pep talk, he'd started to wonder if he really was dismissing what could be genuine interest on Linc's part. Not that it would hurt any less if Caylee was wrong.

The phone rang just before he was about to leave for class. "Courtwright Ranching and Energy. How can I help you?"

"We're still on for Wednesday night, aren't we?" Just Linc's voice was enough to send a shiver up Jonah's nerves.

"I'll tell my instructor tonight that I'll have to miss class," Jonah answered. "What time should I be ready?"

"It runs from seven to ten or so, though we don't have to stay the whole time, just make an appearance. Maybe we can go out for dinner afterward, since they never serve more than cocktails and finger food at these things."

"I'd like that," Jonah said. *See? Linc doesn't just want to be with you only when Melissa's around*, Caylee's voice whispered to him. "What time do you want me to be ready?"

"I can pick you up around six, but you'll have to give me your address."

At six on a Wednesday evening, Wes might be working, but Aidan and Sammy would both be home. The idea of having to face them while Linc picked him up like a prom date was more than a little scary. "You can just come meet me at the office. I can get ready here, and that way I won't have to leave early to drive home and get dressed."

"You know, it's all right if you leave work early, Jonah," Linc said with a hint of a chuckle. "Hell, take the whole day off if you want."

"I don't need a whole day to get ready!" Jonah protested. "Besides, Ford promised to send me the information on the additional breeder cows you're selling by the end of the day tomorrow, and I'll have to get the records updated." *And if I don't have something to keep me busy all day, I'll go crazy from nervousness.*

"Have it your way. Six o'clock at the office." Maybe it was his imagination, but he thought Linc's voice sounded deeper. "I'm looking forward to it."

"I—I am too." It was at least partly the truth.

AT five forty-five Wednesday afternoon, Jonah stood in the restroom in the hall outside the office, staring into the mirror and trying to see himself as Linc might. The black suit fit him as perfectly as Sammy had assured him it would. It was easily the nicest outfit Jonah had ever worn, so at least he wouldn't embarrass Linc by the way he was dressed. He ran his palms over his short brown hair. He'd had it trimmed yesterday after work, and even though he never got much in the way of a five-o'clock shadow, he'd shaved before he changed clothes to be on the safe side. His green eyes looked wider than normal, but that was as much apprehension as anticipation. He slipped the watch Linc had given him onto his wrist and checked the time. *As ready as I'll ever be*, he thought to himself as he gathered his few toiletries into his kit bag to leave in his desk drawer.

He nearly ran into Linc in the hall when he turned from locking up the office.

"Well, don't you clean up nice," Linc said, the way his gaze lingered on Jonah enough to make him blush.

Jonah could say the same for Linc. He'd seen him in a jacket a few times when he'd left from the office for a date with Melissa, but he'd never seen him dressed as formally as he was tonight. The dark charcoal-gray suit showed off his lean physique, the crisp white shirt accenting the tan he never quite lost from working outside. His tawny hair had been freshly cut and styled—he must have made the appointment himself, since Jonah hadn't—and Jonah had never seen him look more handsome.

"Let's see if you say that when the bills come in," Jonah said, hoping Linc hadn't caught him staring. *At least I wasn't quite drooling.*

Linc just laughed and gestured him toward the elevators.

JONAH couldn't help but stare when Linc turned onto Armstrong Parkway. He knew Highland Park was one of the most exclusive—and expensive—neighborhoods in Dallas, but he'd never seen homes like these before. They looked like castles or French chateaus or brick versions of Southern mansions with soaring marble columns. Linc pulled into the drive of a sprawling Tudor-style building with mullioned windows and exquisite landscaping. A valet stand had been set up in front of the path leading to the entryway. The attendant's expression curdled when Linc got out and handed him the keys to the pickup, and Jonah smothered a giggle.

"What?" Linc said as he took Jonah's arm to escort him up the walk.

"That's probably the oldest vehicle he'll park all night."

"I'm not about to rent a Ferrari just to impress some car jockey."

Which was just one more reason Jonah was falling in love with him. They reached the door, and Jonah took a breath. "Do I look all right?" he asked, wishing he didn't need the reassurance.

"There's just one thing missing." Linc reached up to cradle Jonah's head in his hands and bent down to bring their lips together.

The kiss shocked Jonah so much that he gasped, and Linc took advantage of the opportunity to trace Jonah's lips with his tongue before slipping it inside. Jonah tried not to moan at the heat that flared through him. He clutched at Linc's shoulders for support as Linc grew more bold, plundering his mouth. Jonah tasted mint and couldn't help but kiss back, his tongue meeting Linc's as the moment spun out of time. Finally Linc drew back with a final nip at Jonah's bottom lip.

"Now you look perfect," Linc said with a smile.

Jonah lifted a hand to his mouth as Linc opened the door. His lips felt swollen, and he wondered if that was what Linc intended.

THE house was just as stately on the inside. Elegantly dressed men and women clustered in small groups throughout several formal parlors, more than a few of them greeting Linc as they entered. Jonah tried to resist looking around to see if he could spot whether Melissa was there.

A waiter approached them with a tray of glasses. "Champagne, sirs?"

Linc glanced at Jonah with a raised eyebrow. "They might have beer at one of the bars, if you'd prefer."

Jonah shook his head. "I'm good, thanks."

Linc accepted a flute and silently toasted Jonah with it, but before he could raise it to his lips, Eloise approached them, with an older man Jonah hadn't met before in tow.

"I wasn't sure you were planning to attend," Eloise said with a hint of accusation. Her gaze flickered over Jonah like a splash of ice water. "You remember your father's friend Franklin Meredith?" Linc nodded to her escort. "Franklin, my stepson Lincoln and his… guest… Jonah Hollis."

Jonah shook Franklin's hand. "Pleased to meet you, sir."

"I was just speaking with Melissa," Eloise observed as if Jonah hadn't spoken. "She's looking lovely, as always. Much too sweet for that crude John Maxwell."

Jonah followed her glance to where Melissa stood in the next room, her blonde hair loose around the shoulders of a clinging black dress with a deep vee neckline filled with sheer gauze. When she rather pointedly turned her back to them, Jonah could see it was cut just as deeply there too.

"I suppose it was kind of you to invite your assistant to accompany you," Eloise continued. "I'm certain an opportunity like this hasn't come his way before."

Which Jonah supposed was a polite way of saying she thought he had no business being there, but Linc put an arm around Jonah's waist and met Eloise glare for glare.

"Jonah isn't here as my assistant," he said. "He's my date."

JONAH didn't know if Eloise was too stunned to come up with a response or simply felt it would be rude to make a scene, but she pursed her lips and turned away, a rather apologetic-looking Franklin Meredith trailing after her. Jonah felt a bit stunned himself. Though he knew that was the impression Linc wanted to make—surely that was why he'd kissed Jonah the way he had before they'd come in, since he'd never shown any interest in kissing him before—it was still a shock to hear him say it so unequivocally. *Almost proudly*, Jonah might have thought if he didn't know better. He couldn't tell whether Melissa had overheard, but if society functions were anything like small towns, the news would be buzzing around the room soon enough.

When Linc's attention was drawn by an older gentleman who wanted to talk with him about his stance on fracking, Jonah excused himself. He needed something to drink, and he needed a moment to make sense of what he was feeling. He'd be proud himself if he really thought Linc was serious about being his date, but despite Caylee's words, the evidence of how different his world was from Linc's was all around him. Oh, he might clean up well enough to appear to fit in, but that's all it was—an illusion. He couldn't let himself forget that.

Spotting a bar set up in an open space between rooms, Jonah made his way toward it. "A glass of sparkling water, please," he asked the bartender.

"Not drinking?" A fashionably dressed older woman in a black lace gown embroidered with twining roses stepped up beside him. The bartender poured a glass of mineral water and set it in front of Jonah before starting to mix something for her.

"I'm not much of a drinker," he admitted. "And I haven't had dinner yet, so it's probably not a good idea for me to take any chances with alcohol."

"A decision more of the people here should make," she observed. "You're a face I haven't seen before. Is this your first time at one of these events?"

First and last, he thought. "Is it that obvious?"

"You haven't done a thing wrong, if that's what you're thinking," she said with a kind smile. "I'm Natty, by the way."

"Jonah," he said, smiling back. "It's nice to meet you."

"I think I hear a bit of Oklahoma in your voice. Oh, don't look so panicked," she added, patting his hand. "I'm from Bartlesville myself."

"I grew up in Oktaha," he admitted.

"See? We were practically neighbors." She sipped her drink. "So I hear you're here with Lincoln Courtwright."

He'd known it wouldn't take long. "Yes, I am."

"I never did like that Melissa Cutler, though that's mainly because she broke my barrel-racing record at the Oklahoma City rodeo by nine hundredths of a second." Natty laughed. "I'm glad you and Linc had the courage to come here together."

Jonah didn't know how to answer that—he certainly didn't feel very courageous at the moment—so he just nodded.

"Besides, us Okies need to stick together. Did you know Carrie Underwood is going to perform at the Cattle Baron's Ball? She's another Oklahoma girl herself."

"From Checotah, I know." Jonah grinned. "Half the girls I grew up with dreamed of trying out for *American Idol* after she made it big."

"Well, I'll look forward to seeing you there." She gave him a kiss on the cheek before walking away, and Jonah smiled. *Maybe it won't be so hard to fit in after all.*

Linc joined him as he walked away from the bar. "I see you lost no time making a friend."

"She's from Oklahoma, like me," Jonah said. "And she didn't have a problem with my being here as your date. I wasn't sure everyone would feel that way." *Especially after Eloise's reaction*, he added silently.

"You have no idea who she is, do you?" Linc asked with a chuckle.

"She said her name was Natty."

"That's Natalie Prestwick. She's one of the organizers of the Cattle Baron's Ball, and she's our hostess for the night. This is her home."

Jonah laughed. "I'm glad I didn't know that before I started talking with her."

Linc smiled and took Jonah's hand. "C'mon, there are a few people I'd like you to meet before we can get out of here and have some dinner."

Chapter Fifteen

"HAVE a taste for anything special?" Linc asked once they'd retrieved his truck from the valet—who Linc tipped despite his supercilious attitude—and navigated onto the street.

"Anything is fine with me," Jonah answered. He'd been too nervous to eat much at lunch, and though he'd sampled a few of the appetizers offered by waiters circulating among the guests at the party, his stomach was feeling pretty empty. "You can probably guess I don't know this neighborhood."

"Half the restaurants around here are all sizzle and no steak," Linc answered. "Still, we're all duded up for the night. We might as well take advantage of it." He turned off the winding residential street onto a busier thoroughfare. Lovers Lane, Jonah read when he saw a sign at the next intersection. He bit back a laugh at the irony of the name. A few minutes later, Linc turned into a commercial plaza and parked in front of a small storefront restaurant. This time Jonah couldn't help but laugh when he saw the name on the red awning—Amore.

"Italian all right?" Linc asked. "I suppose I should have checked first."

"I love Italian," Jonah assured him. At least it didn't look like the kind of fancy place where he'd have to worry about which fork to use. The inside, though, had an altogether different feel. It was much smaller than he'd expected, with soft lighting and small tables topped with candles and fresh flowers. The kind of place someone would take a date.

"Believe it or not, the worst is actually over," Linc said after the hostess seated them and gave them menus. "The ball is a lot more casual than tonight was. There will be more people, but that means it's louder, with less chance for long conversations. And you'll know people there."

"I will?" Jonah opened the menu, glad to see standard Italian dishes and reasonable prices. "Natty—Mrs. Prestwick—said she'd look forward to seeing me there, but she might have been just being polite."

"Ford will be there, and some of the other folks from the ranch. And we won't have to wear these monkey suits." Linc loosened the knot of his tie and opened the top button of his shirt. "Never feel like I can take a full breath all done up like that."

Jonah had a sudden image of slipping the tie from under Linc's collar and undoing the rest of his shirt buttons. Would his chest be smooth or covered in hair?

Fortunately for his composure, their waiter came up at that moment to take their order.

"What's good?" he asked, since he hadn't done more than glance at the menu.

"Trust me?" Linc asked with a smile.

When you look at me that way? Absolutely. His mouth too dry to speak, Jonah nodded and sipped at his water.

"Two house salads, the veal piccata for him, and the veal and shrimp marsala for me," Linc ordered. "And a bottle of the Ruffino Riserva Chianti, please." The waiter murmured his approval of the order and bustled off. "I'm not much of a wine snob, but I like a nice glass of something red with Italian food."

"I'll give it a try," Jonah said, "though I'll have to take it easy since I still have to drive home from the office."

Linc frowned, but before he could say anything, the waiter returned with their salads and a basket of small, delicious-smelling rolls dripping with melted butter and fresh minced garlic. Jonah popped one into his mouth and moaned when the rich flavor hit his tongue. He was reaching for another when his hand bumped Linc's over the basket.

"Sorry!" he exclaimed. "They're really good, and I guess I'm hungrier than I thought."

"Don't apologize," Linc said. "I like seeing someone enjoy their food. Melissa always just picked at hers—" He broke off, and since Jonah didn't know what to say, they sat in silence until the waiter returned with their wine.

"Tell me about your weekend," Linc said after the bottle was opened and poured. "Did your friend enjoy her birthday?"

Parts of it, Jonah hoped, though he still felt a bit guilty over being the cause of Caylee breaking up with Jack. He didn't want to try to explain that to Linc, though, so he settled for saying, "We had a very nice dinner together." Realizing that sounded a bit abrupt, he added, "Caylee's such a fantastic person. I wouldn't have stayed in Oktaha as long as I did if it wasn't for her. I still wish she could have come to Dallas with me."

Linc sipped his wine, and the waiter brought their entrees soon after, giving Jonah a respite from trying to make conversation while they began eating.

"This really is delicious," he told Linc after a few bites of the savory, lemony veal over angel-hair pasta.

"I thought you'd enjoy it."

"So tell me who else from the ranch will be at the ball," he said, and they spent the rest of the meal talking about the people Jonah would meet there.

After mutually deciding they were too full for dessert, Linc paid the bill and offered Jonah one of the mints the waiter brought back with the receipt. As they walked outside to the truck, Linc said, "I'll take you back to the office and follow you home."

"I didn't have that much wine," Jonah protested, "and it's not very far. I'll be fine to drive."

"I'm sure you will, but I don't want to take any chances. Humor me. Besides, this way I'll know where to pick you up the night of the ball."

It didn't seem worth arguing about, so Jonah agreed. The ride back to their office building went quickly, and Linc idled next to Jonah's truck until he got inside, buckled up, and started the engine. Then Linc followed him on the short drive to the townhouse.

Jonah had expected Linc to be sure he got home safely and then drive away, but he pulled his truck behind Jonah's and parked. They both climbed out at the same time and stood on the sidewalk in front of the building.

"Thank you again for coming with me tonight," Linc said.

"It was my pleasure." It was the standard polite response his mother had taught him, but Jonah realized he actually meant it. Any opportunity to spend time with Linc was special, but for all his misgivings, it had turned out to be a surprisingly enjoyable evening. "It really was."

"I'm glad." Linc took a step closer, and Jonah swallowed. Was Linc going to kiss him again? He suddenly wished he'd taken another mint from the bowl at the restaurant. He'd probably taste like garlic, and—

Linc gently touched his lips to Jonah's, and Jonah lost the thread of any coherent thought. Linc kissed him softly, little moist kisses over different parts of his mouth that didn't demand anything but weren't enough to satisfy Jonah's longing for more.

"Please," he whispered, raising his arms to Linc's shoulders. Linc wrapped his arms around Jonah's back and drew him nearer, opening his mouth over Jonah's. The fruitiness of the wine and the tang of the mint and even the richness of the garlic blended into the most addictive flavor Jonah had ever tasted. He couldn't get enough of it, angling his head to give Linc more access while he let his own tongue explore in turn. He slid his arms down Linc's back, wanting him even closer, until he was standing between Linc's legs, so lost in the moment that he didn't even care that Linc could surely feel his arousal.

Jonah wasn't sure how long they stood there kissing before Linc raised his head. "That's going to have to last me a while," he said quietly. "I'm not sure when I'm going to be able to get back into the office. We'll be rounding up all the cattle starting this weekend so we can vaccinate the calves. The chips make them easier to locate, but there are still plenty of them to track down and inoculate."

One of the things Jonah had learned during his visit to the ranch was that organic certification didn't mean cattle couldn't be vaccinated against diseases. The Broken Spoke used microchips rather than traditional branding to identify its herds, which also made locating individual cattle easier. It was still a huge job, though, and Jonah knew Linc was enough of a hands-on rancher to want to be involved himself rather than just leaving it to his ranch hands. That wouldn't make not seeing him for the duration any easier.

"I wouldn't be any good on a horse, but if there's anything I can do from the office to help, let me know," Jonah offered.

"Just keep on top of the proposals for the new gas leases while I'm tied up with this," Linc said. "I'll call you at least a few times a week to see how things are going." He kissed Jonah again for a long moment and then stepped away. "I better get going." Jonah didn't say anything, and Linc didn't head for his truck. Finally he pulled Jonah in for one last kiss. "You are too damned tempting. Go on and get inside now." Jonah didn't move, and Linc swatted his ass. "Git!"

Jonah walked slowly to the front door with Linc watching him the entire way. Not until he closed the door behind him did he hear Linc's truck start up and drive away.

"So," Wes said from the darkened living room, "just friends, huh?"

"JO, you look fine," Wes assured him for the fourth time as Jonah twitched at the collar of his white shirt. "And you're going to scuff up those fancy boots if you don't stop pacing. I thought you said you weren't as nervous after the donors' party."

"I'm not nervous about the ball—at least, not too much." Jonah glanced out the window for any sign of a Ford pickup heading down the street. "I just haven't seen him in almost two weeks. What if he's changed his mind about whether this is a good idea? Just because Natalie Prestwick didn't have a problem with him bringing me to the Underwriters' Party, maybe the people at the ball won't be as accepting."

"From what you told me, there are going to be thousands of people there. You won't be under the spotlight the way you were at the party. And since when do you care what a few random strangers might think about you anyway?"

"I care what they think about Linc. That's the whole purpose behind all of this."

"Even if it started out that way—and I'm not sure I believe that anymore—it's way more than that now." Wes ran a hand through his hair, making it stand up even more than usual. "And don't give me that 'just a friend' bull again either. I'm your friend, Jo, and no offense, but there's no way I'd kiss you the way Linc did. See?" He pointed at Jonah. "Just thinking about it's making you blush. That was *waaay* more than a friendly good-night kiss."

Jonah could feel the heat when he raised his hands to his cheeks.

"And maybe you haven't seen him for ten days—not two weeks—since the party, but he's called you every afternoon, right? You can't have had that much business to talk about."

"We did—"

Wes raised an eyebrow, and Jonah subsided. There hadn't been anything romantic about the phone calls. Jonah had filled Linc in about any situations that needed his attention or decision, and Linc had told him how the roundup was going—not just the number of calves they'd vaccinated each day, but little funny incidents like the cow that wouldn't let anyone but Ford near her calf. Since Linc phoned when they'd finished for the day, Jonah had taken to staying late at the office so as not to miss him, and each call had gotten longer until Jonah wound up skipping the first hour of his Wednesday-night class. "You can't go risking your grade just to jaw with me," Linc had scolded him, but Jonah treasured every minute of their conversations. He'd been achingly aroused at the end of each call, and in his dreams at night, he relived the kiss they'd shared, though in his dreams they didn't stop at kisses.

"So don't tell yourself this is just a favor for a friend, because everyone but you can see it's more than that for both of you." Wes reached into his back pocket and handed something to Jonah. "Here, put this in your wallet."

"Wes—" Jonah protested when his fingers closed around a condom. "I'm not—"

"Maybe not tonight, but when the time is right, you'll be ready." Wes pulled Jonah into a hug. "You'll know when it is. And now I think I hear a truck pulling up outside."

Chapter Sixteen

JONAH hastily stuffed the condom in his wallet before Wes opened the front door. Like the day at the ranch, Linc wasn't dressed all that much differently than he would be for the office. His jeans might be newer, and his boots were shined, but he wasn't wearing a flashy rodeo buckle or even a hat. Still, there was something about the way he carried himself that sent a flare of awareness zinging through Jonah's senses, telling him—as if he needed any convincing—that he was about to ride off with the ideal of masculine perfection.

Linc seemed almost as struck by Jonah. "You're looking mighty fine," he said after a moment of silent appreciation. "Ready to do some two-steppin'?"

Jonah swallowed around his dry throat and nodded, taking a step forward. Linc took his hand, and they both stood for a moment, lost in each other's eyes, until Wes cleared his throat.

"You kids have fun, now," he said, holding the door open for them. "Don't do anything I wouldn't do."

"And that would be what, exactly?" Jonah teased, grateful to Wes for breaking the moment, or there was no telling how long he might have stood there drowning in Linc's potent gaze.

"Point taken," Wes acknowledged. "I won't wait up."

They hadn't gotten past the doorway when the front door to the other half of the townhouse popped open. "My, don't you look fine as all get-out?" Sammy exclaimed. "Aidan, love, find my phone. We need some pictures."

Jonah might have protested, but Linc smiled and draped an arm around him, drawing him back against his chest. Just a whiff of his subdued cologne was enough to melt Jonah's knees, and he leaned back against Linc's warmth while Sammy snapped photos like it was a fashion shoot.

"Enough, babe," Aidan said finally, taking the phone from Sammy's hand. "They need to get going."

"Our baby's leaving the nest," Sammy cooed, pulling Jonah forward enough to wrap him into a hug. "You have your phone? I want photos from the ball too." Jonah patted his back pocket in confirmation. "And you"—he pointed at Linc—"make sure this young man has plenty of chances to shake his exceptionally fine tail feathers!"

"They are that," Linc agreed, "but Aidan's right. We should get going."

"Say hi to my cowboy for me," Wes called as Linc led Jonah to his truck, and Sammy blew them a kiss.

"Sorry about that," Jonah murmured once Linc pulled away from the curb. "They can go a little over the top at times."

"They're your friends," Linc said. "No apologies needed. Now come sit over here like you know me."

Jonah happily scooted across the bench seat to nestle against Linc's side.

LINC'S level of sponsorship must have included VIP parking, because he was able to bypass the line of vehicles waiting to turn into the Gilley's lot and drop off his truck at another valet stand. The attendant there didn't turn up his nose at Linc's vintage Ford, though that might have been influenced by the folded bill Linc slipped him along with the keys.

"You ever been to Gilley's before?" Linc asked as they passed under the marquee, topped by an enormous neon sign in the shape of Texas, and into the two-story brick building.

"No," Jonah answered. "I wasn't expecting something this big."

"It's a bit touristy for my tastes, but it's one of the few indoor venues big enough to accommodate the ball."

They stopped at a reception table, where a volunteer glanced at Linc's tickets and handed them a pair of gift bags. "The VIP baron party has already started," she said apologetically, "but I believe a number of your group have already arrived. You're at table thirty-six, right up front near the stage."

Jonah glanced in his bag, which was filled with boxes and smaller bags and envelopes. Maybe Sammy would enjoy going through the contents later. Linc took his hand and guided him down a hallway lined with saddles and huge posters of early Western films. "Did they take over the whole place for the night?" he asked.

"Yep." Linc pointed to several signs hanging from the ceiling. "There's a silent auction and a live auction, if that interests you, and some gaming tables if you're a gambler, and of course, you can ride the bull if you're so inclined."

"I'm no gambler, and I'm definitely not a bull rider," Jonah demurred.

"Neither am I," Linc said with a grin. "That's the one event I was never suicidal enough to try, though Ford wasn't half-bad when he put a mind to it." They passed several smaller event rooms set up with covered tables and open bars before reaching the doors for the South Side ballroom.

"This is enormous," Jonah exclaimed as they walked inside. The huge space held hundreds of round, draped tables arranged around a large central dance floor. As they approached the far end of the room, where a raised stage dominated the entire back wall, the tables were cordoned off and numbered. Before they could find thirty-six, Ford spotted them and stood to catch their attention.

"Glad you could make it," Ford said once they'd woven through the tables and groups of people standing around talking. "Missed all the free drinks at the VIP party."

Eloise, who was seated across the table with the same gentleman who had escorted her to the Underwriters' Party, frowned at them but said nothing. Linc reached across to offer his hand. "Franklin, good to see you again. Eloise, thank you for representing the Courtwrights, as always."

Jonah recognized Marcela from the ranch kitchen sitting next to Ford, but he hadn't met the other people at the table. "Anyone who doesn't know him yet, this is Jonah," Linc said by way of introduction. He didn't say Jonah was his date, but he wrapped an arm around Jonah's waist, earning another frown from Eloise. "Jonah, this is Ignacio, the assistant ranch manager, and his wife, Abril." Jonah smiled at them. "And this is Eli, who coordinated the vaccinations for us this year, and Zoe, one of our best calf wranglers."

Eli half rose and offered a hand across the table. Jonah wondered whether Eli and Zoe, or Ford and Marcela, for that matter, were couples or just fellow ranch employees, but it felt rude to ask. "Wes says hello," he told Ford instead.

"You should have brought him along," Ford said with a grin. "We coulda squeezed in another chair for him." He gestured toward a row of catering tables set along a side wall. "Food's not half-bad. You should probably get some now before the place fills up when they open the general admission lines."

"We'll check it out. Grab a couple of beers and some sparkling water for us?" Linc asked, and Ford nodded his agreement and headed toward the line at the nearest bar.

"Hungry?" Linc asked, not moving his arm from Jonah's waist as he steered him toward the food tables.

The way his stomach was tying itself in knots, Jonah wasn't sure he could eat anything, but it probably wasn't a good idea to dance all night—as he fully hoped he would—on an empty stomach, so he agreed. He took a little bit of everything from the variety of dishes offered and did his best to eat as much of it as he could, while behind them a local band took the stage as a warm-up act for the headline performers.

The noise level in the room rose as more people began filling the tables and lining up for drinks,

especially once the band began playing. As soon as
Jonah pushed his still half-full plate away, Linc rose
and offered his hand. "Would you like to dance?"

Since Linc hadn't actually given a direct answer
when Sammy all but ordered him to dance with Jonah,
as much as he'd hoped Linc planned to dance, Jonah
hadn't been completely sure he would. "I'd love to,"
he agreed quickly, taking Linc's hand and ignoring
Eloise's glowering stare as they walked out onto the
dance floor.

It took him a few minutes to get the hang of doing
the two-step with another man, and more than a few
until the warmth of Linc's hand clasping his and his
palm resting just below Jonah's shoulder grew from
a tingle of nervous apprehension to a glow of sensual
awareness. Linc guided him around the floor with
just a slight press of a hand or a nudge of his knee to
indicate the change of direction. By the second dance,
Linc was turning them so Jonah wasn't always stepping
backward, passing the lead between them and back
effortlessly.

Jonah lost count of the dances, the music merging
seamlessly from one song to the next. They walked
back to the table when the band left the stage for
another, more nationally known group, and Jonah took
the opportunity to snag one of the bottles of water Ford
had brought from the bar, along with several bottles
of beer, from an ice bucket in the center of the table.
He snapped a few pictures for Sammy with his phone
and waved when he spotted Natalie Prestwick sitting
nearby, and she blew him a kiss. Eloise wasn't at the
table, but Jonah didn't care if she was dancing with
Franklin or visiting with friends, as long as she wasn't
there scowling at him. He and Linc hadn't gotten any

awkward stares or rude comments while they were dancing—none Jonah had noticed, anyway—and he didn't intend to let Eloise's disapproval spoil his enjoyment of the evening.

During the next set, they joined in several line dances with Ford and the other Broken Spoke ranch hands, but for most of the time, Jonah danced with Linc. It was hard to exchange more than a few words between songs, but the smile on Linc's face and the warmth in his eyes convinced Jonah he was enjoying himself as much as Jonah was.

By the time the third band took the stage, and Jonah had downed his third bottle of water, he needed to find a restroom. Finding lines at all the facilities inside the ballroom, Jonah decided to wander down the hall to one of the smaller event rooms in the hope that one of them would be less crowded. When he was finished, he spent a few minutes watching as people rode the famous mechanical bull, the way it bucked making him glad Ford wasn't among them. He headed back to the main ballroom, but before he got to their table, he spotted Melissa walking up. She wore a creamy silk blouse tucked into a short black leather skirt, a large rhinestone-encrusted buckle on her belt, and what Jonah could swear were the same caiman-skin boots Sammy had tried to convince him to try on during their shopping trip. Her escort was nowhere in sight, which may have been why she didn't hesitate to walk up to Linc and put her arms around his neck.

Jonah was too far away to hear what she said to Linc, but it was clear what she wanted when she pulled him out onto the dance floor. Jonah had been careful to keep a discreet distance between himself and Linc as they danced, but Melissa felt no such compunction. She must have waited until she recognized a slower song that would let her drape herself against Linc through the steps of a country waltz. Jonah walked to the table while following their progress around the dance floor, only to discover someone had taken the last bottle of water. He picked up a beer and sipped it as he watched them dance. Whatever Melissa hoped to accomplish, Linc didn't seem to be going along with it. She might be clinging to him, but he kept his hands on her shoulders and his head up, and as soon as the song ended, he drew away. They exchanged a few more words, but when Linc headed back to their table, she turned and disappeared into the crowd.

A few minutes later, Carrie Underwood took the stage, and Jonah forgot all about Melissa when Linc took his hand and led him back to the dance floor. The music turned slower and more romantic, and Linc slowly lessened the distance between them with each song.

Jonah closed his eyes and let the movements of the dance and the scent of Linc's cologne and the heat radiating from Linc's body lull him into a sensual haze. Linc bent his head until it rested against Jonah's, close enough to feel the rasp of Linc's stubble against his cheek, making Jonah imagine the brush of more intimate skin. Carrie started into a rendition of Patsy Cline's "Crazy," and Linc's lips ghosted over Jonah's ear, his warm breath making Jonah tremble.

When the song ended, Linc murmured in Jonah's ear, "Come home with me."

Chapter Seventeen

JONAH lifted his head to look into Linc's eyes. They seemed darker than usual, and Linc held Jonah's gaze with a potency that wouldn't let him lower his head. "Is it almost over?" he asked, finding it hard to catch his breath.

Linc shook his head, still holding Jonah's gaze. "It goes all night. They serve breakfast for folks who stay that long. But we need to get out of this crowd soon or I'm going to kiss you right in the middle of the dance floor."

Not that Jonah would have minded, but Linc raised a hand to cradle his chin in a callused palm. "And that's too beautiful to share with a room full of strangers."

On any other night, Jonah might have hesitated, but Linc's words couldn't have expressed his own emotions any more perfectly. Jonah needed Linc to kiss him, and he already knew kissing wasn't going to be enough. He'd danced with men before, kissed them before, but he'd never felt the desire to go further, never felt the yearning that heated him through and that he knew, to the depth of his soul, only Linc could assuage.

"Let's go," he said. Propriety whispered that they should say good-bye to the rest of their group, but just this once Jonah was willing to ignore his parents' lessons. Linc didn't even look back at the table, just took Jonah's hand and led him off the dance floor and toward the exit. Jonah thought he saw Ford smile at them from where he was dancing with Zoe, but they were out the door and heading down the hall before he could lift a hand to wave.

Jonah wasn't sure how they made it to Linc's condo. They must have retrieved the truck from the valet and driven the few miles to the Design District and climbed the stairs to his condo on the top floor, but the only things that registered to Jonah were the warmth of Linc's hand in his, the passion shimmering in his eyes, the soft brush of his lips against his hair.

When the door closed behind them, Jonah reached up and pulled Linc's head down to his. He opened himself to Linc's kiss, burying his hands in Linc's hair to hold him in place, not that Linc was making any move to escape. Angling his head so he could delve deeper into Jonah's mouth, Linc worked a hand behind Jonah's head to cushion it, brushing the thumb of his other hand down Jonah's cheek. That gentle touch, even more than the passion of their kiss, set Jonah trembling.

Linc drew back, though he didn't lower his hand. "Too much?" he murmured.

"Not enough." Jonah glanced around Linc's shoulder at the apartment, which was furnished in a modern style that didn't seem to match Linc's tastes. There was a couch, though, which was all Jonah cared about at the moment. He reached up for Linc's hand and pulled him forward until they could sink down onto it.

"Jonah." Linc put an arm around Jonah's shoulder, supporting him while he brought their lips together. The kiss was slow and achingly sweet, but still not enough to slake Jonah's need. He slid his hands over the planes of Linc's back, and Linc hummed against Jonah's mouth. The idea that his touch could give Linc pleasure was an intoxicating one, and he repeated the caresses with his fingertips and then, daringly, drew a palm around Linc's side and between them to brush over his chest. Linc arched his back to give Jonah access without breaking the kiss.

Granted tacit permission, Jonah set in to explore. Using both hands, he stroked upward from Linc's ribs to his collar and back down to his belt. When he drew them up again, he coasted over the tight nubs of Linc's nipples, and Linc groaned. The soft cotton of Linc's shirt was suddenly an intolerable barrier to Jonah's need to feel Linc's skin. He glanced up at Linc while he searched by touch until he found the top button of Linc's shirt.

Linc raised his head from the kiss, his eyes glittering. "Hell, yes," he rasped. "Touch me."

Jonah's fingers might have shook a bit sliding the first button through its hole, but he undid the rest blindly, holding Linc's gaze. Not until he felt Linc's belt against his hands did he glance down at the prize he'd revealed. Linc's chest was dusted with a light coat of golden hair. Jonah pushed his shirt panels aside to uncover the dusky nipples poking out of the curls. He ran the pads of his thumbs over them, and Linc shuddered.

Under his jeans, Jonah's cock was straining almost painfully, not from Linc touching him but from him touching Linc. He circled Linc's nipples with his fingertips, catching a few of the curled hairs and tugging them lightly, then flattened his palms and ran them over the warm, soft skin. Linc let him explore for a few minutes, but when Jonah returned to rubbing over his nipples, he exhaled sharply and drew Jonah back into a kiss. He shifted on the narrow couch at the same time Jonah tried to reach behind Linc to pull his shirttails free, the combined movements almost enough to dump Linc onto the floor.

He caught himself with a palm to the carpet and sat up with a laugh. "The damned place came furnished, and it never seemed worth the effort to change things, but this couch has definitely got to go." He rose to his feet and offered Jonah a hand. "We'll be much more comfortable in the bedroom."

Jonah let Linc help him stand and leaned in for another kiss before Linc led him by the hand into the next room. He knew he was taking a step there would be no drawing back from, but he didn't feel a moment's hesitation. Everything he was feeling told him this was right. This was what he'd been searching for. Linc was the man he'd dreamed of finding all his life. And after tonight, he could begin to believe that Linc felt the same.

The bedroom was furnished in the same modern style as the living room, dominated by a king-sized bed. Linc pulled the rest of his shirttails free and dropped the shirt onto the floor, then sat on the edge of the bed and toed off his boots. Jonah did the same before turning to face Linc.

"Let me see if you're as perfect as I've imagined you," Linc murmured. He trailed kisses down the side of Jonah's face and neck while he slipped open his shirt buttons. Jonah didn't have as much hair on his chest as Linc did, just a diamond-shaped whorl between his nipples that narrowed to a fine line over his abdomen and disappeared beneath his slacks. Linc nuzzled the pulse that pounded at the base of Jonah's throat and then raised his head. "Absolutely beautiful."

Jonah ached for Linc to touch him, but instead Linc slid to the floor and knelt between Jonah's knees. He slid his arms around Jonah's waist and arched him forward until he could move his mouth over Jonah's chest. Jonah's breath caught, and he braced himself on his palms to keep from collapsing into a puddle. Nothing he had ever imagined felt as wonderful as Linc's lips and tongue tracing his ribs, dipping into his navel, nipping up the flat of his sternum. When Linc slid his tongue over a nipple, Jonah couldn't bite back a moan, and when Linc took it between his teeth and sucked at it, Jonah's cock jumped so hard he was sure Linc must have felt it.

Linc ran a palm up Jonah's leg and rested it over the straining denim. "Is this what you want, Jonah?" He didn't stroke, didn't squeeze, but just the heat of his hand was enough to make Jonah fight the urge to come.

"I want you." As tight as his throat felt, he was surprised the words made it out as clearly as they sounded. "Please, Linc."

"Then let's get you out of these." Gently Linc unbuckled Jonah's belt and unfastened his zipper. Jonah pushed up with his hands to let Linc slide his jeans and boxers over his hips and off. While Linc stood to strip out of his own clothes, Jonah pulled off his socks and scooted up to the center of the bed, then took off his watch and set it on the nightstand. He couldn't help but stare when Linc straightened and crawled up the bed to join him. The same fine golden hair that covered his chest coated Linc's arms and legs and formed a halo around the base of his erect cock. Linc had called him beautiful, but Jonah knew he'd never see a more perfect man. He opened his arms and Linc moved into them, and for the first time, Jonah felt the contact of skin against skin over the whole length of his body.

He shivered as Linc's weight settled over him, and Linc eased up onto his elbows. "Too heavy?"

"Just right." Jonah drew Linc back down onto him and into a kiss. He could feel the stir of Linc's cock as he deepened the kiss, and he slid his arms down Linc's back and lower, over the muscular globes of his ass. When he pressed them even closer, Linc groaned and raised his head from the kiss.

"How do you want to do this, darlin'? Bottom or top?"

For a moment Jonah was wholly stunned. When he'd dreamed of being with Linc, it was of Linc taking control, of driving Jonah so out of his mind that he'd do anything Linc wanted. The idea that Linc might offer to give him control had never even entered his thoughts. It wasn't at all an unwelcome idea, but there was no way Jonah would risk their first time together being anything less than perfect by fumbling around, not knowing what he was doing. Of course, that meant admitting his inexperience to Linc. He didn't think it would make a difference, not now, but it was still embarrassing to admit this was his first time.

"You'd better top. I've never done this before."

"You've never topped before? No offense, but the men you've dated must have been idiots."

"No, I—I mean, I haven't—there haven't been—I've never—slept with anyone before."

Linc seemed slightly stunned himself. "You dated girls before you came out?"

Jonah shook his head. "It seemed wrong to lead someone on when I knew I'd never be attracted to her. And since I came to Dallas, well, I've done some clubbing and dated a few guys, but there's never been anyone I wanted to be with that way. Until you."

Linc let out a breath and kissed Jonah tenderly. "My sweet, sweet Jonah. You are a pure-dee treasure." His eyes sparkled wickedly. "And I aim to make your first time one you're never going to forget."

Linc proved to be a man of his word. He knelt over Jonah's body and worshiped it from head to toe, with his hands and then again with his lips and tongue. Whenever he found a spot or a caress that made Jonah whimper, he'd move on to something else and then return to it, keeping Jonah soaring on a sensual high without ever giving him what he needed to tip into orgasm. Jonah tried a few times to return some of the pleasure Linc was giving him, but Linc would allow a brief kiss or touch and then guide Jonah to lie back again and redouble his efforts to set Jonah teetering on the knife-edge of release.

And still it wasn't enough. Jonah had brought himself to climax before when he needed the relief of an orgasm—especially since coming to work for Linc—but it had always been a quick jerk-off. He'd never tried, never even imagined how much more potent it would be to draw out the buildup. Or maybe the difference was that it was Linc touching him, kissing him—loving him. Because that was what it felt like. The touch of his own hand had never made

Jonah feel as if his entire body was one sensitized nerve quivering with bliss. Trying to compare the fumblings of any of the handful of men he'd danced with or even dated with Linc's touch was like—he couldn't even find a comparison, because there was none. Surely Linc had to care for him to take the time to love him so unselfishly and so thoroughly.

Linc had Jonah gasping and moaning and arching into his every touch, but Jonah needed more. No matter how delirious Linc was making him feel, there was a hollowness inside him demanding to be filled. He ached to feel Linc claim him, joining with him in the most intimate of ways. "Please," he pleaded when Linc was crouched between his knees, licking at his cock and occasionally lapping behind it, each swipe of his tongue leaving Jonah clenched in yearning. "Linc, please. I need you."

"You'll never have to beg, Jonah." Linc slid forward and kissed Jonah deeply, letting him taste a hint of his own muskiness that Jonah found surprisingly mouthwatering. Sometime, he promised himself, he was going to taste Linc the same way, but it seemed tonight was not going to be that night. Breaking the kiss, Linc stretched to open a drawer on the bedside table. He set a foil-wrapped packet next to Jonah—who smothered a laugh at the thought that Wes had been right after all—and knelt back between Jonah's knees with a small, curved bottle.

Jonah had tried fingering himself a time or two, but it had never felt particularly good. It had certainly never felt the way Linc's fingers did, ghosting over his crease and circling his pucker, making him quiver with each pass. The liquid was warm and slippery, and he found himself longing for Linc to slide inside him long before he was finally breached with one long finger. He pushed up into the feeling of fullness, eager for more. Linc chuckled softly and twisted the finger until it brushed over something that made Jonah gasp. He bit his lip to keep from crying out, but Linc stretched forward to kiss him gently. "Don't hold back. Let me hear you."

He gave up trying to control himself after that, letting the moans and pleas fall unchecked while Linc prepared him, being careful to rub over that spot whenever the stretch bordered on pain. When Jonah was sure he was going to come if Linc didn't stop, he grabbed him by the shoulders and pulled him up into a fierce kiss. "No more. Now."

Linc handed him the condom. "Put it on me?"

His hands were trembling so badly, it took Jonah three tries to get the package open. Linc closed his eyes when Jonah rolled the condom on. Then he poured a handful of lube into Jonah's palm and guided him in slicking him with it. When Jonah would have lingered, Linc rolled him onto his side and bent one of his knees.

"It'll be easier for you this way, the first time," Linc murmured into his ear. He spooned behind Jonah, kissing the side of his neck as he aligned their bodies. "Let me inside, darlin'."

If there was any discomfort, Jonah couldn't feel it over the wonder of Linc filling him. Linc moved slowly at first, but when Jonah pressed back against him, he grasped Jonah's hip with one hand and stroked his cock with the other in time with his thrusts. Some of the lube still clung to Linc's hand, letting it glide over Jonah's heated skin, and each time he pushed in, he brushed over Jonah's sensitive spot, until Jonah was shaking and crying out Linc's name and nothing, nothing could keep the wave of ecstasy from breaking over him. He was vaguely aware of Linc stiffening behind him, and then Linc was kissing him and wiping him with a warm, wet cloth and drawing him into his arms.

Jonah nestled with his head on Linc's shoulder and let himself drift into sleep, sure that life couldn't be any more perfect.

Chapter Eighteen

JONAH woke slowly, reluctant to leave the dream in which he snuggled against a warm chest, fine hairs tickling his cheek. Something brushed his shoulder, and he swatted it away, nestling closer into the sheltering arms of his fantasy. When a gentle, lingering kiss coaxed his lips apart, his eyelids fluttered open, and he found himself looking into Linc's hazel eyes.

"You're a dream," he muttered sleepily.

"So are you, but it's time to wake up." Linc claimed another kiss. "We both hit the hay hard last night. I thought you might want to shower this morning."

"Don't wanna move." Jonah tried to pull Linc back down with him, but Linc slid out of his grasp and kissed his nose.

"I see you're not a morning person. I'll have to remember that."

"I usually am, but someone wore me out last night," Jonah retorted, then slapped a hand over his mouth when he realized how that sounded. "Dancing, I mean," he added quickly and turned his face into the pillows.

Linc chuckled. "I guess that means I get the first shower." He leaned over and whispered in Jonah's ear. "You could join me."

That sent all kinds of images racing through Jonah's mind, but he didn't dare take Linc up on it. He'd die of embarrassment, if his legs didn't give out on him first at the sight of Linc's incredible body dripping with water. He shook his head but kept it buried in the bedding, sure his cheeks were flaming.

"All right, sleepyhead. I'll be back in a bit—" He nipped at Jonah's ear, which was the only part sticking out of the covers. "—and if you aren't awake by then, I'll have to take drastic action."

Jonah peeked out from beneath the sheet to watch a very naked Linc head into the bathroom. That was definitely a sight worth waking up early on a Sunday morning for. He settled back into the pillows and wondered what he'd done to get this lucky.

He must have dozed, because the ringing of a phone startled him awake. It wasn't his cell—that was still in his pants pocket, wherever they'd wound up on the floor. He pushed up on an elbow and saw a phone flashing on the nightstand. After a brief debate over whether he should answer it, he decided that if someone who had the number for Linc's condo was calling this early, it must be important. He picked up the handset and pressed the Answer button. "Hello?"

There was no response. "Hello?" he tried again. He was about to chalk it up as a wrong number and hang up when a voice spoke.

"I suppose I should have expected to find you there."

He had no problem recognizing Eloise Courtwright's disdainful tone. "Then you shouldn't be surprised that I answered the phone," he replied. Yes, it was a bit impolite, but he was tired of putting up with her attitude.

"Let me speak with my stepson."

"He's in the shower." As soon as he said it, Jonah realized he should have just responded that Linc couldn't come to the phone at the moment. The fact he was still there told its own tale, but Linc's showering surely betrayed the intimacy they'd shared.

"You think you've won, don't you?" Eloise scoffed. "You ignorant little fool. Surely you can't imagine this was anything more than a means for Linc to punish Melissa?"

"Punish her? For what?" That didn't make any sense to Jonah, and besides, Linc would never deliberately set out to hurt anyone.

"For her behavior at his office. Melissa knows she mishandled that badly. No man likes to have his hand forced that way. His father was no different." She gave a dismissive *tsk*. "So he invited the most outrageous 'date' he could find in her place. Even that foreman of his admitted it. 'Linc couldn't have found anyone more sure to put a burr under that—'" She broke off quickly. "'—under her saddle.' I heard him say it to one of the other ranch hands."

Jonah could believe Ford had said that—he certainly would have used an epithet for Melissa that Eloise wouldn't care to repeat. And he knew, from his eavesdropped conversation, that Ford had urged Linc to find a date—any date—to take Melissa's place.

"Melissa tried to apologize at the ball, but it was impossible to hold a conversation on the dance floor," Eloise went on.

That was true enough, as Jonah had learned—and he'd seen Melissa pull Linc into a dance and try to talk to him.

"So I've invited her to join Linc and me for dinner at the ranch tonight. They'll work through this misunderstanding, and everything will go back to way it should be."

"Linc doesn't want to see Melissa anymore. He said so," Jonah protested.

"Of course he'd say that to you," she snapped dismissively. "Do you honestly think for a moment that Linc would rather have attended the ball with you than with Melissa? You may not have heard the sniggers and jeers about his bringing another man as his guest, the way you were clinging to him like a tick all night, but I assure you, I did. You were there for one reason and one reason only. And now he no longer needs you. Linc would never do anything to permanently disgrace the Courtwright name and reputation."

Jonah's stomach was starting to roil. He hadn't heard anyone make disparaging comments last night, but they'd spent most of their time around Ford and the others from the ranch. Had his being there really hurt Linc's reputation?

"And don't get the idea that his spending the night with you means anything. Why do you think he keeps that condo in the first place?" Eloise sneered. "It's where he brings the men he picks up to sleep with. He may think I don't know his dirty little secret, but I'm not blind. At least he knows better than to bring that kind of sick behavior to his home. You're just the latest in a very long string, and he didn't even have to go far to pick you up, did he? It's clear you were all too willing to fall into his bed. And now that you've served his purpose of getting back at Melissa, he'll drop you just as fast as all the others."

Jonah was afraid he was going to be sick. The memory of how aggressive he'd been last night—kissing Linc as soon as the door closed behind them, all but dragging him to the couch, putting his hands all over him—what must Linc think of him? How could he possibly face Linc after the way he'd behaved?

Eloise was continuing to spill poison into his ear, but Jonah couldn't listen anymore. He dropped the phone back into its cradle, scrambled out of bed, and hunted around the floor for his clothes—one more bit of proof, if he needed any more, of how out of control he'd been. He pulled them on with trembling hands and stumbled out of the condo, desperate to get away before Linc could ask him to go.

He was on the sidewalk outside before he remembered he hadn't driven and didn't have a way to get home. Surely he could find a cab? He didn't see one, so he just started walking in the general direction he thought was south, Eloise's words echoing in his head: *Now that you've served his purpose of getting back at Melissa, he'll drop you just as fast as all the others.*

She was right. He'd known better. He'd known all along this was just a charade, but like the ignorant fool Eloise called him, he'd let himself believe that it could be real. *Stupid, stupid, stupid.*

JONAH didn't know how long he spent walking
blindly. When the sun beating down on him started to
make his head throb, he looked around and realized he
had no idea how to get home from wherever he was.
There was almost no traffic, nothing but warehouses
and businesses that didn't seem to be open on Sunday.
Finally, in desperation, he pulled his phone from his
pocket and called Wes.

It must have been late enough in the morning by
then that Wes answered after a few rings. "Jonah? Hey,
you get lucky last night after all?"

Jonah almost sobbed. "Wes, can you pick me up?"

He must have sounded terrible, because Wes's
teasing voice turned instantly serious. "Are you okay?
What happened? Where are you?"

He could see construction cranes and highway
overpasses ahead of him and walked back to the nearest
intersection to read the street signs. "Dragon Street and
Wichita?"

"Okay, stay there. I'll check Google Maps and
come get you. Is everything all right?"

Nothing was right, but he couldn't explain it over
the phone. "Just hurry."

He found some shade under a tree bordering a
parking lot and hunkered to the ground, letting his head
fall to his knees. The more he remembered his behavior
last night, the sicker he felt. It had been beautiful, but
he'd been so selfish, letting Linc do all the work to
please him. And as soon as they finished, he'd fallen
asleep. Even if it had meant anything, Linc would never
want him in his bed again. Linc had promised to make
his first time one Jonah would never forget, and he'd

succeeded. As much as Jonah wished he could erase the memory from his mind, he knew the night's humiliation would stay with him forever.

He couldn't just sit there whining like a child. He had to move, had to get away. Jonah struggled to his feet and was about to start walking again—somewhere, anywhere—when Wes pulled up on his scooter.

"Are you all right? What happened? Did he hurt you?" Wes demanded.

Jonah just shook his head. Trying to explain what a fool he'd made of himself was more than he could deal with.

"Because I swear, if he hurt you, I don't care how rich he is, I'll kick his ass—"

Jonah swallowed around his dry throat. "Just take me home, Wes."

Wes gave him a searching glance, as if checking to be sure he didn't have any injuries, then handed Jonah his spare helmet. "You'll have to hang on. I couldn't bring your truck because I can't drive a stick."

"It's okay, Wes. Thanks." Jonah strapped the helmet on and climbed on the scooter in back of Wes. It wasn't really meant for two people, but Jonah wrapped his arms around Wes's chest and buried his face against his back, grateful that the rush of wind as they rode made conversation impossible. The contact might have been soothing, except it made him remember waking up pillowed against Linc's chest, and he started to feel sick again.

When Wes pulled up in front of the townhouse, Jonah climbed awkwardly off the scooter and headed inside. He went straight to his room and pulled out his duffel bag, then started throwing in T-shirts and jeans and underwear at random. He should shower, should change clothes, but that would take time, and all he wanted was to get out of there.

He nearly walked into Wes in the doorway. "What the hell is going on? You're scaring me, Jo. Sit down and talk to me."

"I made a fool of myself," he said when he realized Wes wasn't going to let him by without an explanation. "I let myself believe it meant something when it didn't."

"What did he say to you?"

"It wasn't him." Jonah sighed. "I just need to go home, Wes."

"You're not driving like this. I'll take you."

"You can't drive a stick, remember? And I'm not riding all the way to Oktaha on your scooter."

"Then I'll ride with you in the truck," Wes said. "I don't think you should be alone."

"I'll be fine once I get moving. Besides, how would you get back here? You have to work tomorrow." Of course he did too, but that was supposing Linc would still want Jonah working for him, or that Jonah could stand going back to the way things were even if Linc didn't fire him.

Wes pulled him into a hug. "I'm so sorry, Jonah. Whatever happened, you don't deserve this. You'll find someone better the next time around."

There wouldn't be a next time, but Wes didn't need to hear that. Jonah hugged him back and then plodded down the stairs and outside to his truck. As much as he knew Wes hurt for him, he needed to get back to the only person who had always loved him unconditionally.

Caylee.

Chapter Nineteen

THE diner was closed by the time Jonah pulled into Oktaha. It was only a little past five, but there wasn't enough business to stay open on Sunday afternoons when almost everyone in town was having supper with their families. The drive had taken him nearly four hours. He could usually make it in less, but he'd been in no real hurry to get back and admit how royally he'd screwed up. He just couldn't stay in Dallas to face Linc, and there wasn't anywhere else for him to go.

As he drove, he realized it was almost laughable how differently the dreams from his childhood had actually turned out. He and Caylee had planned to shake the dust of Oktaha from their feet and see the world together. When they'd come home for visits, everyone would exclaim over how well they were doing, and anyone who'd ever taunted him would have to eat their words.

Instead he was slinking back with his tail between his legs. The only exotic places he'd seen were Dallas and Linc's ranch. He'd mingled with the upper crust of society a time or two and fooled himself that he might ever fit in with them. Though he'd never really cared about fitting in with them—only about being with Linc. And he'd managed to wreck any chance of that because he couldn't keep his hands to himself and his dick in his pants. As a teen, he'd never really paid much attention to his parents' lectures about the risk of giving in to arousal, since he'd never imagined himself feeling that way about anyone. He supposed he owed them an apology.

He never should have agreed to Linc's charade. He'd told himself it was only to help Linc and that he could keep his longing for Linc hidden. Linc would never have to know. But he'd been lying to himself. He'd have done anything just to be able to spend the time with Linc. Except that Linc was so kind and attentive that he'd let himself believe Linc was starting to care for him too. And last night, when Linc was parading him in front of Melissa to show her what she'd thrown away, he'd deluded himself into believing it was real. He'd let the music and the closeness arouse him and hadn't had the sense to realize that was all it was. Linc would have been a fool not to go along when he'd all but thrown himself at him. But now Jonah couldn't deceive himself any longer. That one night with Linc was all he'd ever have.

The fact that he'd lost his heart in the process didn't matter. At least Linc would never know that. He'd reconcile with Melissa, or find some other nicer woman to marry and give him the children he needed to continue the Courtwright legacy. And Jonah would go back to Oktaha and cry on Caylee's shoulder and then find some way to go on.

Without Linc.

HE drove the few blocks to Caylee's apartment—in reality a few rooms the Beltons, the family who ran the feed store, had turned into a separate space for Mrs. Belton's mother to live in and had rented out after her passing. It had its own entrance at the back end of the house, a fact Jonah was grateful for since it meant he wouldn't have to face the Beltons. It would be all around town soon enough that he was back; he didn't need Mrs. Belton to start the phone tree this quickly.

He parked the truck alongside the house and tapped on Caylee's door. It took a moment or two before it opened a crack and she peeked out to see who was there. When she recognized him, she gave a squeak and threw the door open wide, then pulled him inside and wrapped him in a hug.

"Jo-Jo, what are you doing back so soon? Never mind, it doesn't matter. I'm just so glad you're here!"

When he'd seen her at the diner two weeks ago, Jonah had thought she seemed run-down, but now she looked even worse. Her face was puffy and her eyes were red, as if she'd been crying, but her skin seemed pallid, and he could swear she'd lost weight. Something was not right. He couldn't unload his own problems on her until he knew what was going on. "Caylee, what is it? What's wrong?"

She gave him a weak smile. "It hasn't been the best few weeks, but what are you doing here? You didn't say anything about planning to come back after my birthday. Is everything okay with your parents?"

"As far as I know. I haven't been to the farm yet," Jonah admitted. "It hasn't been the best few days for me either, but never mind that for now. Tell me why you've been crying."

"Not until you tell me why you're back here out of the blue like this," she insisted. "You haven't been home since Christmas, and all of a sudden you're here twice in a few weeks, and no offense, Jo-Jo, but you look like hell."

"And you look like you're sick! Are you?"

Caylee laughed. "Listen to us, bickering over which one of us looks worse. Let's call it a draw, okay? I'm not up to a fight."

"Then tell me what's going on, Cay."

"If you tell me what's going on with you."

He'd never been able to win an argument with Caylee. "Okay, but you go first."

She drew in a breath and exhaled. "Let's go sit down. I have a feeling this isn't going to be a short conversation."

He followed her to the love seat in the small living area, and they sat, but she didn't say anything. He'd never known Caylee to hesitate to speak her mind, which made him even more worried. He took her hands in his and squeezed them. "Spill."

She took another breath and held it. "I slept with Jack Ballinger."

It wasn't funny, but he had to laugh. "And I slept with Linc Courtwright."

"But that's good, right?"

He shook his head. "Not so much. You?"

"Not so much." They both grinned at the weak joke.

"I mean, the sleeping part—actually the part before we slept, though that was nice too—it was beautiful, but I practically forced myself on him—"

Caylee poked him on the arm. "I'm sure he wasn't putting up much of a fight! Why wouldn't he want to make love with you?"

Jonah had to blink back the sudden sting of tears. "I thought that's what it was, Cay, but the next morning…. It was all just to make Melissa jealous. I knew that going in, but I'd wanted him for so long, and when I really got to know him over all those lunches and dinners, it was so much stronger than just superficial attraction. And then at the ball, we spent almost the whole night dancing, and it was so perfect I forgot it wasn't real. I wanted him to love me, so much…. But it wasn't going to be more than that one night, and I couldn't stay there and face him after that."

"Did he tell you that?" Caylee's eyes flashed with indignation.

"No, but he didn't have to. His stepmother called this morning, and she's already working on getting him and Melissa back together. She said Linc's being at the ball with me was hurting him socially, and he'd never do anything to permanently harm the family name. And now that I'd served my purpose, he didn't need me anymore."

"I'm sure that isn't true, Jo." Caylee squeezed his hands.

"She said—" Even the memory hurt, but he needed Caylee to hear it all. "She said I shouldn't think it meant anything that he slept with me, since he took all the boys he picked up to his condo. That I was only the latest in a long line, and I didn't mean any more to him than they had."

"And what did Linc say to that?"

"What difference would it make? She was right. Even if Linc did feel anything for me, all it would do was hurt his reputation."

"Did Linc tell you that?"

Jonah shook his head. "I couldn't face him. After the way I'd come on to him, and—" Not even to Caylee could he admit he'd let Linc pleasure him and then fallen asleep. "I left while he was in the shower."

"Jonah David Hollis! Do you mean to tell me you walked out on the man without hearing his side of the story?"

"I *couldn't*, Cay. I couldn't stay there and listen to him thank me and pat me on the head and send me home." He swallowed back the tightness in his throat. He wouldn't let himself cry, not even in front of Caylee. "I couldn't let him see that I'd fallen in love with him when all he'd wanted was a favor from a friend."

Caylee pulled him into a hug, and he let himself lean on her for a few moments before he straightened. "So now you know why I look so terrible. What's your excuse?"

He'd hoped to lighten the mood, but Caylee didn't smile. "I'm pregnant."

For an instant Jonah thought she was teasing him in return, but her expression didn't change. "And don't you dare ask me how."

"I grew up on a farm, Cay. I know how. But weren't you using protection?"

Caylee flushed. "It wasn't something we planned. We just—it happened before we realized it."

Before last night, Jonah might have challenged that, but he had his own experience now of letting desire sweep him into something he hadn't meant to happen.

"Jack hasn't been with anyone else, and based on my time of the month, I thought I was safe." She shrugged. "Then I was late, and I started losing my breakfast."

That explained why she looked so pale and worn down. "Have you seen a doctor?"

"Who, Doc Snyder? I might as well paint it on the water tower in six-foot letters. And you know the closest hospital's in Muskogee. I had to drive to Warner on my day off last week just to buy a home pregnancy test from a drugstore where no one knew me."

"Does Jack know?"

Her expression hardened, and she nodded. "Once I was sure, I told him." A tear trickled down her cheek. "He's already started dating Ella Kilmer. He doesn't want anything to do with me or the baby. He offered to pay for an abortion, but I can't—"

This time Jonah drew Caylee into his arms and held her until her tears slowed. She pulled a tissue from her pocket and blew her nose, then shook her head.

"I'll manage on my own somehow. I'm just not sure how yet. I don't know if the Beltons will let me stay once the baby's born, but anywhere I'd move to would be more expensive. I'd have to see if I could work more hours at the diner, though I'll have to pay for daycare too, unless the Littells let me bring the baby to work, and there's no way I'll be able to take any classes...."

Jonah wished he had a solution to offer, but he knew Caylee was right.

"And the worst part is that everyone in town is going to be gossiping about what happened. I don't care what they say about me, but I hate the thought that this little baby"—she rested a hand on her abdomen, which wasn't showing anything yet, though Jonah didn't know how much longer that would last—"will have to grow up without a father or even a father's name. You know how cruel kids can be," she said sadly.

"Not just kids," Jonah added. "We're a pair, aren't we?"

"We had such big dreams." Caylee sighed. "And instead of making it out of Oktaha, I'm stuck here as an unwed mother, and you're back with a broken heart. We deserve each other."

"Who else would have us?" Jonah stopped suddenly as an idea dawned on him. It wouldn't do anything for his broken heart, but it could be the solution to Caylee's problems.

"I know that look, Jo-Jo. What wild scheme have you come up with?"

"Caylee," Jonah said solemnly, "will you marry me?"

Chapter Twenty

"**MARRY** you?" Caylee didn't quite laugh in his face, but it was a near thing. "Jonah, first of all, you're gay, remember? And second, you're in love with someone else."

"Someone who's never going to love me back." It didn't get any easier to say, but he had to face reality. "Think about it, Cay. You're my best friend in the world. There's only one other person I'd consider spending my life with, and since that's not going to happen, why shouldn't I spend it with you?"

"Because you don't want to get married?"

"But it would solve so many problems." Jonah took Caylee's hands. "You could come live with me on the farm, so you wouldn't have to pay any rent. You know my mom has wanted us to get together more than anything. I'm sure she'd be thrilled to watch the baby while you work or take classes, so you wouldn't have to worry about daycare. I can find another job, either with the trucking company or somewhere, and I could still work on my business degree part-time."

"What about your job in Dallas?"

Jonah couldn't let himself think about that. "I'll give my notice. It would be too awkward"—*too painful*—"to stay there after this, anyway."

"You make it all sound so easy," Caylee said. "But you'd be giving up so much for me, Jo-Jo, and what would you get in return, besides a wife you don't want and another man's baby?"

"It's *your* baby, Cay," Jonah insisted. "You'd be giving me something I never thought it would be possible to have in my life. And this way he or she wouldn't grow up without a father. I'd be proud to give it my name." Even if no one in town believed the baby was his, he didn't think anyone would be crass enough to say so to their faces. "And if you find someone later who loves you the way you deserve to be loved, someone you really want to spend the rest of your life with... I wouldn't stand in the way."

Caylee raised her hands to his cheeks. "The same would be true for you, Jo-Jo—*if* I decide to accept your oh-so-flattering offer."

There wouldn't be anyone else, Jonah knew, but it wasn't worth arguing about. "As if I'd meet someone here in Oktaha. We won't be giving up our dreams, Cay, just putting them on hold for a little while. We'll still make it out of here someday—together this time."

"Maybe you should talk with Linc before I say yes," Caylee said. "Hasn't he tried to call you at all since you left?"

"Ummm…." Jonah frowned. He'd tried to avoid giving any thought to having to face Linc again. "I don't really know. I think I put my phone in the duffel bag with the clothes I packed." If you could call stuffing the first things he laid his hands on "packing." He was lucky he'd brought the phone along at all. The last thing he'd wanted was to talk with anyone during the drive home.

Caylee bopped him on the side of his head. "Go get it and see, Einstein."

"I hope the baby doesn't inherit your vicious streak," Jonah muttered as he headed to the door. Rather than digging around in the truck, he brought the whole duffel inside and dumped its contents on the love seat. The cell phone bounced off the cushion and fell to the floor.

Jonah retrieved it and pushed the button to wake the screen. Nothing happened. He pressed the Power button to be sure he hadn't turned it off accidentally. Nothing. "It's dead."

"Well, plug it in."

Jonah riffled through the pile of clothing. "Uh, I didn't bring the charging cable. Can I borrow yours?"

"You could, but it wouldn't do you any good. You have an iPhone. I have an Android." She grinned. "The parts won't fit."

He stuck his tongue out at her. This was why he'd needed to get to Caylee. Maybe it was juvenile humor, but she had him smiling again. "I don't suppose my parents have bought an iPhone in the last two weeks?"

"You know your mother. 'What would I use a cell phone for? We never go anywhere but to town and back. And if I have to call someone there, the phone we have works perfectly well.'"

"Okay, then." Jonah tossed the phone into his duffel and piled the clothes back on top of it. "If anyone did try to call, I guess I wasn't meant to know about it." A part of him wondered if Linc had tried to get in touch with him after he'd left—after he'd run away, to be honest—but the greater part of him wouldn't let himself give in to more useless hope.

Caylee frowned. "I still think you should talk to him."

"It won't change anything, Cay, but I'll call him from my parents' house." He didn't add that he'd be calling the office to leave a message on voice mail that he wouldn't be coming back to work. It wasn't like he had Linc's cell phone number, anyway. In fact, he was fairly sure Linc didn't have his cell phone number either. He remembered having to list it on his employment records as an emergency contact, but did he really think Linc would have gone into the office on a Sunday to track it down? If he was lucky, Linc would follow his usual pattern of not coming into the office until Wednesday, and he wouldn't even know Jonah was gone until then.

"See that you do," Caylee insisted.

"Scout's honor." Jonah held up three fingers. "So how about it, Cay? Are we going to get married?"

"I shouldn't even be considering it." She sighed. "I'm not saying yes, but I'm not saying no either. Go home to your parents' and sleep on it. I mean really think it all through, Jonah. We both wound up where we are by acting in the heat of the moment. This is too important to make the same mistake. If you still feel the same way in the morning, call me."

"I won't change my mind, Cay."

"Then you can call me when you wake up. I'll be here, losing my breakfast before I go in to work."

Jonah stood and pulled her into his arms. "I love you, Caylee Lynch."

"You know I love you too, Jonah. I just want us both to be sure we're doing the right thing."

He bent his head and gave her a gentle kiss. He wouldn't let himself compare it to the kisses he'd shared with Linc.

She leaned into him for a moment and then straightened. "Go home and get some sleep."

"I'll talk to you in the morning."

HIS mother was just setting supper on the table when he walked into the kitchen. She was so clearly surprised by his arrival that she nearly dropped the platter of roast chicken. "Jonah! We didn't expect to see you again so soon. Is everything all right?"

Once she set the platter down, he gave her a hug and nodded to his father, already seated at the head of the table. He was about to answer automatically that everything was fine, but of course it wasn't. Realizing he really should have thought about what he wanted to tell them before he got there, he quickly edited the truth. "I decided Dallas wasn't for me." Not for the reasons his parents would think, but he didn't have to admit that. "I've decided to move back to Oktaha."

"Oh, I'm so happy to hear that." His mother beamed at him from across the table. "Sit down and let me get another plate. There's plenty of food."

Since she always cooked at least twice as much as they'd ever managed to eat in a single meal, that was a given. "I'll get it, Mom. I still remember where everything is."

He fetched a plate and silverware and took the chair next to his father. Once they'd all served themselves, his mother smiled at him and said, "I hope this is a result of your birthday dinner with Caylee. I knew nothing in Dallas could compare to what you've had waiting for you right here at home."

Caylee had hardly been sitting around pining for him, or he for her, but it would be easier to let his mom believe that than to try to explain the real situation. "I stopped to see Caylee on the way here." After taking a deep breath, he added, "I've asked her to marry me."

"Oh, Jonah!" She jumped up and came around the table to hug him. "That's such wonderful news! Isn't it, Ben?"

Jonah's father raised an eyebrow. "Did she say yes?"

"Not yet," Jonah admitted. "She wants us both to sleep on it, but I hope she's going to accept."

"And why wouldn't she?" his mother demanded. "It was her mother's dearest wish. And Caylee couldn't find a better man than you in all of Oklahoma."

That was wrong on so many levels, but denying it wouldn't serve any purpose. "If she says yes, I'd like to bring her here to the farm to live, at least to start."

"Well, of course you'll both live here! Your father can use the help, and I can teach Caylee all the little things about keeping a house that her mother never had the chance to before she passed."

His father frowned, but as much as he might dislike the implication that he needed help, Jonah was sure he could use it. At least until they could replace some of the older haying equipment with more modern, automated models.

"There's something else," he said after a moment. It was really Caylee's secret to tell, but even if she didn't agree to marry him, it wouldn't stay a secret much longer, and as much as he was sure his mother would be overjoyed at the news, he needed to be sure before he volunteered her services. "Caylee's going to have a baby."

His mother raised both hands to her mouth, as if she was trying to hold back a cry of joy. "Oh, Jonah! I knew all this nonsense about your being attracted to men was just a phase you were going through! Though I shouldn't condone intimacy before marriage, this is such wonderful news that I can forgive you. Did you hear, Ben? We're going to be grandparents!"

The expression on his father's face was less than ebullient, and Jonah felt guilty about the deception, but since he fully intended to raise Caylee's child as if it were his own, he didn't see anything to be gained by confessing the truth now. Once the baby was born and they'd had a chance to love it for its own sake, it would be easier for them to accept the situation.

He hoped.

"You wouldn't mind watching the baby some, would you, Mom?" he asked instead. "Caylee and I would both like to go back to college, at least part-time, and that way we wouldn't have to try to find daycare."

"As if I'd let some stranger watch my grandchild." His mother stretched a hand across the table to him. "I'm so happy for you, Jonah. I always knew you and Caylee were meant for each other."

His father narrowed his eyes but said nothing.

AFTER supper, Jonah helped his mother clean the kitchen and listened to her chatter about plans for the wedding and setting up a room for the baby and looking for his old crib in the attic until he was forced to remind her that Caylee hadn't said yes yet.

"As if she's going to turn you down!" She hung her dishtowel and turned to cup Jonah's face in her hands. "I knew God would hear my prayers in his own due time."

Guilt turned his stomach into a rock. "Mom—"

"Your father and I are going to get ready for bed. Dawn seems like it comes earlier every morning. But you can stay up as late as you like. Just turn the lights off when you come up to bed." She kissed his cheek. "You've made us so very happy."

After his parents went upstairs, Jonah brought the duffel bag in from his truck and then stared at the old-fashioned beige phone on the kitchen wall. He'd give anything not to have to make this call, but he owed Linc that much, at least.

He picked up the handset and dialed the number from memory, listening to the clicks as each digit was counted out. When the recording of Linc's voice announced that Courtwright Ranching and Energy couldn't answer his call at the moment, he nearly hung up the phone, but he forced himself to swallow and wait for the beep.

"This is Jonah Hollis." *Stupid*, he berated himself—Linc knew his last name. "I'm calling to say that… that I won't be coming back to work. I'm sorry not to give any notice, but…." What reason could he possibly give? *But I love you too much to work for you anymore?* He swallowed again and forced out, "I hope you find someone to replace me soon. Thank you for… for everything." His voice caught, and he hung up, unable to say anything else.

He picked up his duffel and trudged up the stairs to his room, already knowing he wasn't going to get any sleep.

Chapter Twenty-One

AS he expected, Jonah didn't get much sleep. The few times he dozed, his dreams were full of memories of his night with Linc, which was even worse. True to his word to Caylee, he spent his waking hours thinking about the proposal. It was still the best solution he could come up with, the only one that offered any kind of positive outcome. Going back to Dallas, trying to return to work as if nothing had happened, flat-out wasn't an option. Linc might let him keep his job, but Jonah couldn't bear the thought of becoming nothing more than an employee again, of having to watch Linc find someone else, of ordering flowers and jewelry for his replacement. No, not replacement, because that implied he'd ever meant anything more to Linc than a way to thumb his nose at Melissa and a one-night romp in bed. At least marrying Caylee would make her situation so much better, and he'd have the comfort of living with his best friend and helping her to raise her child.

As soon as the first rays of sunlight teased at his bedroom window, he got up, washed and brushed his teeth, and dressed in jeans, a denim shirt, and his old boots. He forced away the reminder of the last time he'd worn them—at the Broken Spoke—and went downstairs to find his parents already in the kitchen.

"There are scrambled eggs and toast and homemade jam." His mother set down plates loaded with food. "No bacon, though. Your father's watching his cholesterol."

Jonah's father scowled. "She made turkey bacon once. Tasted like shoe leather."

"You should taste the meatless Spanish frittata my roommate, Wes, makes for our friend Sammy. You'd never guess there's no sausage—" The realization of how much he'd miss Wes, Sammy, and Aidan dried the words in his throat. He owed Wes a phone call, after leaving him with no real explanation. He'd have to drive back to Dallas in a week or so to pack up the rest of his things and give Wes a check for the next few months' rent. It was the least he could do to make up for leaving him without notice. It would eat up most of his savings, but once he found a job in Oktaha, he could start to build it up again. He had one more paycheck coming from Courtwright Ranching; fortunately his check was directly deposited into his bank account, so he wouldn't have to go in to the office to pick it up or make arrangements to have it forwarded in the mail.

They finished eating in silence. Jonah's father rose and kissed the top of his mother's head. "I'll be out in the barn. Jonah, I'd appreciate a hand when you're done in here."

Jonah nodded, then helped his mother clear the table. He dried and put away the dishes she washed and then excused himself to call Caylee.

The coiled cord on the handset of the phone was long enough to stretch into the next room, so he dialed her number and walked into the parlor for a little privacy. When the call rang eight times with no answer, Jonah started to worry that Caylee hadn't been joking about getting sick in the morning. He walked back into the kitchen, where his mother was taking ingredients out of the cabinets for some kind of baking.

"If you're trying to call Caylee, she's probably at the diner already. She starts work at six. There's a magnet on the refrigerator with the number."

"Thanks, Mom." Jonah dialed again but didn't bother leaving the kitchen this time. He'd never been able to keep anything from his mother for long. No use trying to start now.

"Oktaha Diner." The voice belonged to Deanna Littell, who owned the diner along with her husband, Russ, who did most of the cooking.

"Mrs. Littell, could I speak with Caylee?"

"Is that you, Jonah Hollis? I heard you were in town a few weeks ago. You stop by when I'm working this time so I can see you, hear? Hang on, let me get Caylee."

Deanna's shout of "Caylee! Jonah's on the phone for you!" came across the line so clearly that he had no doubt everyone having breakfast knew he was calling. Oh well, they'd know everything else soon enough.

"You sleep any, Jo-Jo?"

Caylee sounded tired, and Jonah wondered how well she'd slept.

"Some. Did you?"

"Enough. Did you call him?"

"I left a message." Jonah lowered his voice. He'd rather not have his mother asking who "he" was. "He hasn't called back."

"You wouldn't know unless your phone's miraculously come back to life. I don't suppose you left him your parents' number, did you?"

He loved Caylee, but sometimes she could be downright annoying. "I told you I'd think about it, and I did. I haven't changed my mind. Please, let's do this, Cay."

The other end of the phone was so quiet he could hear the clatter of silverware against plates. Finally Caylee said, "Yes. I'll marry you."

There was a whoop from someone in the diner, quickly cut off.

"You won't regret it, Cay, I promise. I'll pick you up after work so we can make plans."

"I can drive over. Tell your mother I'll bring some of that Salisbury steak your dad likes so much for dinner."

"I will. Love you, Cay. See you soon."

He hung up the phone and turned to face his mother, who was giving him a searching look from where she stood by the table.

"Well?"

"She said yes."

"I knew she would! Oh, Jonah, you've made us so happy!" She drew him into a hug and kissed his cheek. "Go tell your father the good news. He won't come out and say it, but I know he can use your help."

When he entered the barn, his father looked up from where he was tinkering with a baler, his gaze no less searching than Jonah's mother's had been. "Are you certain you want to do this, son?"

While his father had never been especially demonstrative, Jonah had expected him to at least seem pleased about the news, certainly not to question it. "I'm doing what both of you always wanted."

"What your mother always wanted. She's so excited about the baby she can't think beyond it." His father wiped his hands on a rag and stepped around the baler. "All I've wanted is for you to grow into a good man, and from what I can see, you have. I can't say I understand your preferences, but it seems to me that trying to be something you aren't isn't going to work out best for anyone."

Jonah was so stunned he didn't know how to respond. This was more than his father usually offered voluntarily in a week's worth of conversations. He'd always just assumed his father shared his mother's sentiments. He ought to have known better.

His father clapped him on the shoulder. "Just be sure you're making the right choice. I'm going to check the west field. See if you can get that baler working again, will you?"

After his father left, Jonah gathered some hand tools and dug into the baler's innards. He'd spent so much time here in the barn as a teenager, imagining he was Luke Skywalker working on a vaporator and dreaming of an adventure to sweep him away from his backwater existence. But to paraphrase another childhood hero, his own adventure had turned out quite differently. It didn't seem likely he could hope for another with a better outcome.

JUST after lunchtime, he'd gotten the baler's jammed augers to spin and was testing the pressure of the bale tension arms when his mother came into the barn.

"Jonah, Caylee's on the phone for you."

"Is something wrong?" He couldn't imagine why Caylee would be calling so soon. Surely she hadn't changed her mind?

"I don't think so, but she didn't say."

He followed his mother back into the house and picked up the phone. "Cay? What is it?"

Caylee's voice was low but urgent. "He's here!"

"Who's here? I mean there?"

"Your boss! Mr. Courtwright."

Jonah's breath caught in his throat. What was Linc doing in Oktaha? A flare of hope that he was there looking for Jonah sparked, but he ruthlessly stamped it out. Still, what else would have brought him there? "What did he say?"

"He came in and ordered an iced tea and then asked if anyone knew where he could find the Hollis farm. I figured out right away who he was—and why didn't you tell me how good-looking he is?—but before I could say anything, Deanna blurted out that I certainly did, since I was your fiancée. Jonah, I have never seen anyone look so shocked in all my life! He turned to stare at me, and I said I had an order to pick up and ran into the kitchen. I don't feel right about this, Jo-Jo. What do you want me to tell him?"

What Jonah wanted was for none of this ever to have happened, but that wasn't a choice. The last thing he wanted was to face Linc—he'd run from Dallas as fast as he could to avoid it—but it didn't appear he'd be able to prevent this confrontation, and it wasn't fair to put Caylee in the middle of it. "Go ahead and tell him how to get here. I'll listen to what he has to say."

"Okay, but he seems pretty upset. I'll see if I can get him to order lunch and calm down a bit first, maybe? I'd offer to drive him myself, but I've got another two hours on my shift, and I don't think I can keep him here that long."

"No, it's good. Thanks for the heads-up, Cay. Love you."

"Love you too."

Jonah hung up the phone. "Mom, there'll be a man coming out here shortly—the man I worked for in Dallas, Mr. Courtwright. Will you send him out to the barn when he gets here?" He didn't know what Linc wanted to see him about, but whatever it was, he didn't want to have the conversation under his mother's eye.

"The barn? We don't entertain guests in the barn! You come up to the house and speak with him in the parlor like civilized people."

Thinking fast, Jonah answered, "It's okay, Mom. He's a rancher—remember I told you he owns a big spread called the Broken Spoke? He's been looking for new sources for feed, and I told him about the farm." *None of that is strictly a lie*, he told his grumbling conscience.

"Then he should speak with your father."

"He's out working the west field. I'll show Linc around and then bring him out to meet Dad."

He could tell her sense of propriety wasn't mollified, but he got her to agree to bring Linc out to the barn when he arrived. "Though I'll at least offer him some coffee or tea before you take him traipsing all over creation, if that's all right with you."

Since he couldn't think of an objection other than *Something tells me I don't want you talking to him*, he said that was fine and went back to fighting with the baler.

Caylee must have convinced Linc to eat something, because it was nearly an hour later before Jonah heard a vehicle pull up in front of the house. He hoped Linc hadn't grilled her with questions, mostly because there was no telling how Caylee might have answered.

His nerves were jumping with anticipation, and it seemed like another hour before he heard the screen door to the house open and then shut, though in reality it couldn't have been more than ten or fifteen minutes. A shadow obscured the light shining in through the open doors of the barn, and Jonah looked up to see Linc standing there, the sun behind him turning his hair to spun gold.

"So," Linc said, his every word dripping icicles, "your mother tells me congratulations are in order."

Chapter Twenty-Two

JONAH had never heard Linc sound so cold, not even when Eloise had been riding him about Melissa. So much for any thought that Linc might have come to bring him back to Dallas. Judging by his voice, Linc was this side of furious. Jonah couldn't figure out why, though. From a day's distance, he recognized that leaving without a word had been immature and rude, but Linc would hardly drive four hours to rake him over the coals for that. So why *had* he come? Jonah had to clear his throat to be sure he was able to speak.

"What are you doing here?" He was thankful it didn't come out sounding too quavery.

Linc dug a hand into the pocket of his jeans, and Jonah dragged his gaze up before Linc could catch him watching.

"You left this on the nightstand when you took off." He held out the wristwatch he'd given Jonah the morning after he'd agreed to accompany Linc to the Cattle Baron's Ball. Jonah had raced out in such a panic, he'd never even realized he'd left it behind.

He reached out a hand, and Linc dropped the watch into it as if he'd burn if they touched.

"After you listened to whatever viciousness Eloise poured into your ear, I wasn't sure if you'd forgotten it or if you left it to send me a message."

"How'd you know—?" Jonah's throat tightened and he stopped short, clutching the watch hard enough to cut into his fingers.

"When I came out of the bathroom and found you gone, the first thing I did was check the phone to see if you'd called anyone to come get you. No outbound calls, but Caller ID showed me the ranch number, and that the call had lasted for a fair spell. I could give a good guess what Eloise said to you, and she was more than happy to fill in the rest when I called her back."

Jonah knew he owed Linc an explanation, but he couldn't move, couldn't speak, as if he were frozen in place by the coldness of Linc's tone.

"I waited awhile to see if you'd come back— thought maybe you just needed a while to think. After an hour or so, I got restless. The concierge desk said they hadn't called a cab for you, so I drove around for a bit to see if I could spot you walking, but that didn't pan out. Then I went to your house, but your roommate wouldn't tell me anything at first. I don't know what he thought I did to you, but I finally got him to admit you'd been there, though he said he didn't know when you'd be back."

Linc ran a hand through his hair. "For some reason I thought maybe you'd go to the office, but there was no sign you'd been there. I looked up your contact records and tried calling your cell phone, but it kept going straight to voice mail. I tried most of the night."

Looking at the dark shadows around his eyes, Jonah wondered whether Linc had gotten any more sleep than he had.

"I thought sure you'd show up for work this morning, but when you didn't, I figured chances were good you'd headed here."

"My phone battery died," Jonah forced himself to say. "I didn't have the power cable to charge it. But I left you a message at the office." He slid the watch onto his wrist and flexed his fingers to start the blood flowing through them again.

"Did you?" Linc's stare was pure ice. "I didn't think to check for one. I spent the drive up here trying to figure out what made you run and how to convince you to come back." He shook his head. "You should have headed to Hollywood 'stead of back to Oklahoma, good of an actor as you are."

"Actor?" Jonah choked out, but Linc kept on as if he hadn't spoken.

"And I bought every line of it, like a damn fool idiot. 'I've never slept with anyone before.' Did you and your *fiancée* laugh about how easy I was to sucker?" Linc's voice somehow managed to sound even colder. "Never been with a man—was that another lie? Or were you just willing to do anything it took to get your hooks in me? 'There's never been anyone I wanted to be with that way—until you.' That was the biggest lie of all, wasn't it? And Lord help me, I believed it all."

Jonah shook his head, struggling to speak. "I didn't—"

"And you know what the real joke is?" Linc sounded like his words were being dragged across broken glass. "You folded your hand too soon. If you'd stuck it out just a little longer, you would have won the whole pot. When I finished my shower yesterday morning, I was going to make sweet love to you again, and then I was going to ask you to marry me. Isn't that a hoot? The ranch, the oil, the gas leases—you could have had them all. Why aren't you laughing?"

He clenched his hands into fists at his side, as if he didn't trust himself not to reach out for Jonah and throttle him. Jonah wasn't sure he didn't deserve it.

"Maybe you overestimated how much influence Eloise has on me, or maybe you just couldn't stand what we did Saturday night enough to put up with the prospect of a lifetime of it. I guess it doesn't matter anymore. You and your fiancée and your baby have a real good life, Jonah."

Linc turned toward the door, and without his glare paralyzing him, Jonah was finally able to move. He grasped Linc by the arm and spun him back around, gripping him by the biceps, and forced himself to meet that frigid stare. "Everything I've ever told you is true. I know it looks bad, but if you let me explain—"

"I've heard enough lies, thank you."

Linc's tone was drier than the dirt beneath their feet, and Jonah knew words wouldn't convince him, so he did the only thing he could think of.

He slid his hands up to Linc's face, cupped his cheeks in his palms, and kissed him.

Linc tried to pull back, but Jonah called on a reserve of strength he didn't know he had to hold him in place. He poured everything into the kiss—his love, his regret, his apology, his desire. He traced his tongue over the slightly chapped contours of Linc's mouth until it opened on a groan, and he took shameless advantage of the opportunity to slip his tongue between Linc's lips. When Linc's tongue met his, a flicker of hope rekindled, and Jonah pulled him closer, angling their heads so he could reach deeper into the moist recesses of Linc's mouth. *Please listen,* he begged silently. *Please let me tell you the truth.*

By the time he had to break the kiss before his lungs burst, Linc was leaning forward to capture his lips again.

"Caylee's baby isn't mine," Jonah managed to say between short, sweet kisses.

"Your mother said—"

"She wants it to be true, so we let her believe it, but—" Linc claimed his mouth again, and Jonah sank into the kiss, too grateful to protest. Explanations could definitely wait as long as Linc was kissing him again. When it was Linc's turn to come up for air, Jonah continued. "Caylee broke up with her boyfriend, who's a homophobic jackass, before she found out she was pregnant. When I thought we were—we were through," he stumbled as his voice broke, "I thought getting engaged to her was the best solution for both of us."

"But what made you think we were through?" Linc's pain was evident, and Jonah wondered how he could have ever doubted what they both felt.

"Eloise said—"

"Eloise fed us both a load of bullcrap," Linc said. "She tried to convince me you were nothing but a gold-digging hustler, but I couldn't believe her, not until I got here and everything seemed to point to her being right." He kissed Jonah again tenderly. "I'm sorry I let her convince me for even that long."

"And I'm sorry I left without talking with you first. It wasn't just what Eloise said," Jonah admitted, feeling himself flush. "I know I wasn't what you expected. I didn't know what to do, and then as soon as we were finished, I fell asleep on you." He turned his head, unable to meet Linc's gaze. "I know I shouldn't have run, but I just couldn't face you again after disappointing you like that."

Linc caught Jonah's chin in his hand and turned his face until their eyes met. "If you thought I was disappointed, God help me once you learn a few things—you'll like to kill me."

"But you had to do everything," Jonah said once he'd caught his breath after Linc's kiss.

"Darlin', if it'll make you feel better, you can do everything next time, and the time after that, and the time after that," Linc said with a wicked smile. His expression sobered a moment later. "There's just one problem. You're still engaged to somebody else."

A bit of Jonah's joy faded at the reminder. "Caylee won't hold me to it. She made me promise that if either of us ever found someone else, we wouldn't stand in each other's way." But when he made that promise, he'd expected it would be Caylee finding someone else. It didn't feel right for him to find his happiness and leave her with all the problems their getting married was supposed to solve. "Except…."

"Except?" Linc echoed warily.

"Except Caylee will still have to raise her baby alone, in a town that doesn't have much of a track record for accepting… alternative lifestyles."

"Hell, that one's easy. She can come live on the ranch with us. If you think she'd want to, that is."

"Could she?" It seemed like an ideal solution to Jonah. "I'd love to have her closer, but you wouldn't mind?"

"Why should I?" Linc shifted nearer, until Jonah was leaning back against the baler with Linc cradled between his legs. "She's your best friend, and I'd love to get to know her better. There's plenty of space on the ranch, and no one there will care who her baby's father is."

"They may still think it's mine—or yours," Jonah cautioned.

"We'll know the truth, and what anyone else thinks doesn't mean squat."

"Caylee's coming here once she gets off work, so we can ask her," Jonah said, wondering if it could really be that easy.

"There's something else I need to ask before she gets here." Linc dug into the pocket of his jeans again, and as close as they were standing, Jonah could feel each pass of his hand, awakening all sorts of delicious feelings.

"I practiced how to say this all the way up here, but then you got me so discombobulated, it all went plumb out of my head. So I'll just have to say it plain. Jonah Hollis, I love you, and I can't think of anything I want more than to spend the rest of my life with you. Will you marry me?"

Jonah's heart felt as if it was going to burst out of his chest. "I've been in love with you since the day I came to work for you. I was terrified you'd find out how I felt and fire me. I never dreamed you'd actually feel anything for me in return. Yes, yes, I'll marry you."

Linc's kiss was slow and sweet, though the way they pressed together left no question that he was as aroused as Jonah was. "This was my father's wedding ring," he said after Jonah finally let him go. "I like to think he'd have approved once he got to know you." He slid it onto Jonah's finger, where it fit as if it had been made for him. "I reckon I can take that as a sign."

Jonah pulled Linc's head back down into another kiss. After all the emotional highs and lows of the past few days, he could hardly believe Linc was really here, kissing him, loving him. He slid his arms down Linc's strong back and lower, pulling him close. Wanting him. Jonah arched his hips, rubbing against Linc as Linc's kiss grew forceful. It felt so wonderful....

"Jonah David Hollis!" His mother's voice trembled with shock. "What is going on here?"

Chapter Twenty-Three

JONAH pulled out of the kiss, and Linc took a step back and angled a bit so he could see Jonah's mother glaring at them, but he didn't move his arms from around Jonah. Which was just as well, since Jonah sincerely hoped Linc's body was hiding the evidence of how aroused they both were.

"Ma'am," Linc said politely, "your son has just done me the honor of agreeing to marry me."

Jonah's mother planted her hands on her hips. "He's already engaged. To Caylee!" She gestured to where Caylee was coming up behind her.

Caylee mouthed a silent "Sorry" to Jonah before putting a hand on his mother's shoulder. "Jonah was trying to help me, Mrs. Hollis. The baby isn't really his," she confessed. "I'm sorry we lied to you, but

I didn't know how much he was in love with Mr. Courtwright or I never would have agreed to marry him." She stepped around Jonah's stunned mother to offer a hand to Linc. "I'm Caylee Lynch, and I think I owe you an even bigger apology, Mr. Courtwright. I did try to get him to call you first, I promise."

Linc unwrapped an arm from around Jonah to take her hand in his. "He can be a bit headstrong, can't he? We'll have to work on that. And please, call me Linc—I have a feeling we're going to get much better acquainted."

"But you're—you're like him?" Jonah's mother asked Linc, apparently dumbfounded by the idea.

"If by 'like him' you mean intelligent, hardworking, principled, and loyal, then not quite, but I'm working on it," Linc replied. "Your son sets quite an example to live up to."

Awed by the sincerity of Linc's words, Jonah turned an adoring gaze on him but was saved from having to respond by the sound of a tractor pulling up beside the barn.

"That'll be your father. We'll see what he has to say about this." She turned to Jonah's father as he entered the barn and demanded, "Tell your son he can't throw his life away by taking up with this—this man rather than Caylee!"

Linc took a step forward—leaving Jonah thankful the confrontation with his mother had eased the tightness in his jeans—and extended a hand. "Lincoln Courtwright, sir, and I mean to marry your son, since he's agreed to have me."

"Ben Hollis." Jonah's father shook Linc's hand and then clapped Jonah on the shoulder. "Glad to see he's come to his senses."

"Ben!" his mother gasped.

"It's legal now, Mary," he reminded her.

"Just because it's legal doesn't make it right."

"Never did understand what part of loving someone can be wrong." He put an arm around his wife and steered her toward the house. "What are y'all standing around in the barn for? Let's go inside and get to know the man a bit better."

"Tell me about your haying operation," Linc asked as he joined Jonah's parents, with a glance over his shoulder at Jonah. Jonah nodded toward Caylee, and Linc winked. "I'm always looking for new sources for feed."

"He's a charmer," Caylee observed as they disappeared into the house. "He'll have them eating out of his hand in no time."

"You really don't mind?" Jonah asked. "This could make things even harder for you."

"I suppose Deanna's let the whole town know by now that we're engaged." Caylee shrugged. "It'll give them something to talk about once you're gone, at least until the next scandal surfaces."

"Or you could come with us," Jonah suggested.

"I'm sure Linc would love that—bringing your ex-fiancée back to Texas with you? The man's clearly crazy about you, Jo-Jo, but I can't see him going along with that."

"It was his suggestion, actually," Jonah assured her. "There's plenty of room on the ranch, and that way I'd still be able to be a part of the baby's life." He took Caylee's hands in his. "I didn't realize how much I want that until just now, when I thought about leaving without you. And if you come with us, you won't have to listen to anyone talking about the baby or the broken engagement or anything else."

"And just what am I supposed to do on this ranch?" Caylee asked, though Jonah could see she was giving the idea some consideration. "I'm not a freeloader or a charity case. I'd have to find a job, and I'd still like to go back to school someday."

"We didn't talk it through yet, but maybe there's something you could do on the ranch for Linc?" Caylee looked skeptical, and Jonah hurried on. "Or maybe you could find a job in a town nearby, or even in Dallas."

"Or maybe I should just stay here, where I already have a job."

"And an apartment you might not be able to stay in, and daycare to pay for, and people gossiping about you behind your back." Jonah squeezed Caylee's hands. "I didn't have any guarantees when I left for Dallas, and look how things worked out. Sometimes you just have to take a chance if you want things to change."

"I don't know, Jonah… I should probably think about it for a while."

"I'm afraid you'll just talk yourself out of it," Jonah said. "We've dreamed about this since we were kids on the playground together, Cay. I don't want to sound mean, but what do you have to stay here for? Now that your mom's gone, the closest you have to relatives are my folks, and you'd be quitting a job at the diner, not some great career. I know it's kind of scary to leave everything you're used to behind, but I'll be there for you." He pulled her into a hug. "I had to leave town without you once already. Don't make me do it again."

Caylee sniffled and wiped her eyes with her hands. "Damned hormones. You are *not* making me cry. I suppose I can give it a try. If I hate it, I can always come back."

"That's wonderful, Cay!" Jonah lifted Caylee off the ground and spun her around. "We can have you packed up and ready to leave tomorrow."

"Uh, Jonah," Caylee said when her feet were back on the ground, "not to burst your bubble, but where exactly are you planning to stay until tomorrow?"

Jonah's smile faded. "Here?" he offered hesitantly and shook his head. "You're right. There's no way I'm not sleeping with Linc tonight, and I can't do that with my parents just down the hall."

"And there isn't room for you to sleep at my place."

"We'll just have to leave tonight, then."

"I'll stop at the Eazy Mart and see if they have some boxes I can use to start packing." Caylee kissed him on the cheek. "Go rescue your fiancé, and come pick me up when you're ready to go."

"You won't be sorry, Caylee." If her luck was half as good as his had proven to be, Jonah knew that was the truth.

LINC might not have had both Jonah's parents eating out of his hand when Jonah joined them inside, but he certainly seemed to have won his father over. The two were deep in a discussion over the relative merits of grass and alfalfa hay and the best proportions to feed wintering beef cattle. His mother was stringing beans from the garden, though by the way her forehead was creased, Jonah knew she was still wrestling with his announcement.

"Caylee brought Salisbury steak from the diner. You can peel some potatoes to mash," she told Jonah.

He realized just sitting down to a meal with Linc represented a significant step for her, and he regretted having to dismiss her overture, though not enough to reconsider spending the night. "We can't stay for supper, Mom. Linc and I have to get back tonight."

Linc looked up with a question in his eyes but didn't voice it aloud. "Yes, we have some business to attend to that can't wait another day."

"You'll have to come back soon for another visit and to let us know your plans for the wedding," Jonah's father said when Linc stood to shake his hand.

"But what about Caylee?" his mother asked worriedly. "Everyone expects you to be marrying her."

"Caylee's coming with us," Jonah said. Linc nodded at Jonah's assertion as if it had all been agreed upon ahead of time. "The Broken Spoke will be a wonderful place for the baby to grow up."

"I don't understand, Ben." Jonah's mother looked as if she was about to break into tears. "If Caylee's going with them, why couldn't he just have married her?"

"There now, Mary. Just think of it as both Caylee and Linc joining the family."

Jonah gave his mother a hug before his father clasped his shoulder. "I'll work on her," he said softly while Linc took her hand in both of his to say good-bye.

Jonah retrieved his duffel bag before he and Linc headed out to the yard.

"We have to get back tonight?" Linc turned Jonah's statement into a question.

"Unless you want me to make love to you with my parents in the next room, yes."

Linc pulled him into a quick kiss. "That's the best offer I've had all year, darlin'. Let's get a move on."

"We have to pick up Caylee first. She's packing her things now."

"I only know how to get back to the diner, so lead the way."

CAYLEE already had most of her clothes packed by the time they got to her apartment. "It's kind of pathetic how little I have to show for myself, isn't it?" she asked, staring at the small pile of boxes. "Most of the furniture belongs to the Beltons, though I would like to take my mother's rocking chair, if one of you can put it in your truck."

"Just think of it as an opportunity to make a completely fresh start," Jonah told her. "We can put the boxes and the rocker in my truck, and you can drive it, if you don't mind." He was looking forward to the drive back to Texas nestled against Linc's side.

"No way, José. I'm not leaving my car here."

"You can't seriously be thinking of driving that rust bucket all the way to Texas, are you?" Jonah looked at Linc for support. "It's that piece-of-junk Chevy Metro out front that's held together with bubble gum and bungee cords. C'mon, Cay, the engine would probably blow out before we hit the border."

"How do you expect me to get around once I get to Texas without a car? And *don't* tell me Linc will buy me one, or you can leave my boxes right here and head back to Dallas all by your lonesome."

"Not all by his lonesome," Linc said with a smile. "Listening to you two, I don't know whether to be happy or not that I don't have any siblings." He ran a hand through his hair. "But we'll be driving a caravan back with two trucks and a car. It's after five now, which means it'll be nine or ten before we get to Dallas, and it's another few hours past that to the ranch. I don't much like the idea of making you try to find it in the dark, especially if there's any chance you might have car trouble. I don't suppose there's a hotel we could stay the night and leave in the morning?"

Caylee and Jonah exchanged glances. "Closest hotel's in Muskogee, and that's heading out of our way north," Jonah said with a frown. "There are some chain hotels in McAlester, about an hour or so south on 69. We could make it to there and then stop for supper and stay the night, I guess." As much as he didn't want to spend the night with Linc at his parents' house, spending it in a hotel wasn't much more appealing, but neither was waiting seven more hours to be together. Or even four, if they stopped in Dallas, though he shuddered at the thought of Caylee having to sleep on the couch of Linc's condo while he and Linc made love in the bedroom, and even more at the idea of the three of them spending the night in the townhouse and having to explain the situation to Wes, Sammy, and Aidan. No, finding the closest hotel was definitely the best solution.

"Let's saddle up, then." Linc leaned toward Jonah and murmured in his ear, "The sooner we get moving, the sooner we can stop."

"If y'all will load up my things, I'll let the Beltons and the Littells know I'm leaving." Caylee grinned. "Just as long as we get two rooms at the hotel—and I think I'll ask to be put on a separate floor!"

Chapter Twenty-Four

IT was after six by the time they left Oktaha. Their little caravan made its way south on US 69 with Linc in front, Caylee in the middle, and Jonah bringing up the rear with Caylee's belongings in the back of his truck. They'd stopped to pick up a tarp to cover the bed so they wouldn't have to unload overnight. Traffic was light, and they were making good time, but Jonah found it difficult to concentrate on the road.

Since he was the last in line, all he had to do was follow Caylee's taillights and let her and Linc regulate their speed, which was fortunate since on his own he would surely have gotten tagged in a small-town speed trap. Even the hour drive to McAlester was too long when his mind kept flashing back to the feel of Linc's lean body pressing his against the baler as they kissed.

He was already hard enough to make sitting on the truck's bench seat uncomfortable. Trying to banish the memory only resulted in his imagination painting pictures of all the things he could do to Linc once they found a hotel and checked in to a room. He might not know much more than he did before Linc made love to him, but he had Linc's example to build on and Linc's promise to let him do everything he wanted—and oh, how he wanted!

More than ever, Jonah regretted leaving behind the charging cable for his cell phone when he fled from Dallas. If he couldn't ride back nestled against Linc, he could at least have talked with him along the drive, even though he knew from experience how arousing Linc's deep voice alone could be. Okay, that thought wasn't helping to reduce his excitement any either. He shifted in his seat and tried to focus on the road ahead.

A few miles out from McAlester, he started spotting billboards for several chain hotels. Though he assumed Linc and Caylee saw them too, he flashed his headlights at Caylee, who tapped her brakes in reply. Jonah didn't care which one of the options they stopped at, as long as it had two rooms available. The sun was close to setting when they reached town, and Linc turned off the road at the earliest opportunity and pulled into the parking lot of a Hampton Inn.

"This work?" he asked when they'd all parked beside each other. The lot had a few other cars but was far from full, which wasn't surprising at just past seven o'clock on a Monday evening, giving Jonah hope they'd have no problems getting two rooms.

Without bothering to answer, he grabbed Linc's hand and all but pulled him toward the hotel's front door.

Caylee followed behind them with a wide smile. "Eager much?" she murmured before the glass panel slid open. Jonah grinned back.

The desk clerk checked them in as if it were the most commonplace act imaginable, which Jonah supposed it was to her. She obviously wasn't picking up on his jittery impatience as she magnetized their room keys and handed them across the desk.

"Thank you, ma'am." Linc slipped his credit card back in his wallet and smiled at her. "Whereabouts would you recommend for getting something to eat?"

When she smiled back, Jonah had to resist the urge to slide his arm around Linc's waist and let her know in no uncertain terms that Linc was taken.

"If you want more than fast food—" Linc nodded, and she paused thoughtfully. "—there's Chinese or Italian just up the access road, but if you want my advice, the best place in town is La Cabaña." She pulled out a local map and circled their location, then made an *X* a few blocks away. "It's nothing fancy, but the food is great. Tell them Lena sent you."

She smiled again, and this time Jonah took Linc's hand as he thanked her before heading back out to the parking lot.

"Feeling a mite possessive?" Linc raised an eyebrow but didn't let go of Jonah's hand.

"Just holding on to what's mine," Jonah answered as Linc opened the driver's door to his truck. Jonah climbed in before Linc could, and Caylee rolled her eyes and got in the passenger side. "I wanted to be here the whole drive down," he added, leaning against Linc once he'd buckled up and started the engine.

"You sure you want to deal with him?" Caylee asked with a grin. "He can be a handful."

"I expect I can learn to put up with it," Linc answered, wrapping an arm around Jonah's shoulders.

The food at the restaurant could have been the best Mexican in the state, but Jonah didn't taste a bite of his enchiladas. Linc got a beer to go with his guisado de puerco, while Caylee ordered flautas and an iced tea. The service was friendly and—more important to Jonah—quick, so that before nine they were back at the hotel. Jonah grabbed his duffel and Caylee's overnight bag from the truck before they went inside. Since Linc hadn't planned to be gone overnight, he had nothing with him. Lena was still at the check-in desk when they entered the lobby, so they chatted for a few minutes about their supper before wishing her a good night and heading for the elevator.

"Same floor, I'm afraid, but at least a few rooms away from each other," Linc said when he gave Caylee her key.

"I have earplugs," she answered with a grin. "Mr. Belton snores loud enough I could hear him through the walls. Just remember the folks next to you might not be so well equipped."

"We'll keep that in mind. Sleep well, and call the room when you're up and ready for breakfast."

"Considering I'm used to working the sunrise shift at the diner, that may be earlier than you're ready for. Don't worry. I'll let you get your beauty sleep." She hugged Jonah. "Have a good night, Jo-Jo."

Despite her teasing, Jonah hugged her back. "Thanks. Love you, Cay."

"I'd be careful saying that with your boyfriend right there, but love you too. Night, y'all."

Their room, once they went inside, was clean and spacious, but the only amenity Jonah cared about was the king-sized bed. He dropped his duffel on the floor, threw the bolt on the door, and turned toward Linc, who opened his arms in invitation.

Jonah walked into them and pulled Linc's head down into a kiss. "Do you know how long I've been waiting to do that?" he asked when they paused for breath.

"Since your mother and Caylee walked in on us, I imagine, since I've been waiting just as long. Now what are you going to do about it? I did promise to let you do everything this time, if you recall."

If Linc thought that would make Jonah hesitate, he was about to learn differently. Jonah pushed him back gently until he was sitting on the end of the bed. "Get undressed."

"Oh no." Linc shook his head with a wide grin. "Everything means everything."

"Fine," Jonah countered, toeing off his boots. He knelt to pull off Linc's and tossed both pair in the general direction of the door. One of them hit the panel with a *thump*.

"Getting noisy already?"

Jonah rose enough to quiet Linc's chuckle by covering his mouth with his own, leaning forward until Linc was recumbent on the bed. He worked his hands between them and undid the buttons of Linc's shirt by feel, but the position was awkward, so he straightened and motioned to Linc. "Scoot up to the pillows and lie flat on your back."

Linc was quick to obey, but when he tried to shrug out of his open shirt, Jonah wagged a finger at him. "Everything, remember?"

"You're the boss." Linc lay back with a smug smile.

He'd expected to feel at least a little nervous, but gazing up the length of Linc's body, Jonah knew exactly what to do. He knelt at the foot of the bed and crawled forward until he was straddling Linc's hips. Leaning down, he captured Linc's lips again, holding Linc's hands down when he would have reached up. "Just lie there and let me love you."

The look Linc gave him was so trusting, so wanting, so loving that Jonah had to kiss him again. When he'd regained his composure, he let his lips roam over Linc's stubbled chin and down the slope of his throat. He could feel Linc's Adam's apple bob when he swallowed, and he closed his mouth around it and laved it with his tongue. Linc moaned quietly, and Jonah could feel the vibration against his lips. A shudder ran through him, and he felt himself hardening.

Jonah shifted on his knees, following the contours of Linc's neck. He traced his tongue over the hollow at the base of his throat but didn't linger—the expanse of lightly furred chest was too enticing. He watched the rise and fall with each of Linc's slightly ragged breaths for a moment, then pushed aside the open shirt panels while he decided where to explore first. The pebbled nipples peeking out of tawny curls were the obvious destination, but he bypassed them in favor of nuzzling his nose through the tickling mat, dropping random kisses. Linc shifted beneath him, and Jonah held his shoulders, letting his teeth come into play with little nips. Each time Linc dragged in a quick breath, Jonah hardened a little more, the idea that he was giving Linc pleasure incredibly arousing. When he finally closed his mouth over a nipple and sucked on it, Linc groaned, and Jonah's cock jumped.

When he'd paid homage to every bit of Linc's chest, he worked open his buckle and unfastened his zipper. The musky scent made his mouth water, and he made short work of stripping the jeans, boxers, and socks down Linc's legs and dropping them on the floor. He considered taking his own clothes off—his jeans were pressing painfully against his erection—but somehow being fully clothed while Linc was naked except for the shirt still over his arms was intensely erotic. Jonah started at Linc's feet and kissed his way up the long, strong legs, moving from one to the other and licking or nibbling as the mood struck him. He discovered the backs of Linc's knees were ticklish but didn't exploit it at the moment, filing the knowledge away for future use. As he got closer to the juncture of Linc's legs, the hums and moans issuing from Linc's throat grew more constant. It was so tempting to close his mouth over Linc's rampant erection, but he had a whole other side still to explore, so he contented himself with a quick kiss to the tip before nudging Linc to roll over.

Linc groaned but complied, holding himself up on his knees so he wasn't smashed against the bedding. Jonah slid his arms out of the shirt one sleeve at a time and added it to the pile of clothing on the floor. Linc threw a pleading glance over his shoulder before settling onto the pillows. Jonah spent a pleasant few minutes kissing up and down Linc's tanned arms before turning his attention to the strong muscles of his shoulders and back. He nipped down the length of his spine, tracing his tongue along each rib. When he reached Linc's firm buttocks, Linc pushed up onto his elbows. "Darlin', have mercy. You're killing me here."

"Roll back over," Jonah instructed hoarsely.

A drop of cloudy liquid trembled on the tip of Linc's cock, and Jonah lapped up its salty taste. He started to slide his lips down its length, but Linc stopped him with a hand on his shoulder. "Too close for that. Tell me you've got a condom?"

"Do we need one?"

"I believe you haven't been with anyone but me, and I've always used protection, but I want us both tested before we do without." Linc kissed him tenderly to take any sting from the words.

Jonah fumbled for his wallet and pulled out the packet Wes had given him. "I came prepared."

Linc chuckled. "Don't suppose you have any lube in there too?"

Jonah peered at the packet. "It says it's prelubricated."

"That won't help any with getting me ready."

Jonah blinked at the easy assumption that he'd be topping this time.

Linc must have read his surprise, because his grin widened. "Everything, remember?"

"Don't you have lube?" Jonah asked.

"I didn't leave Dallas hoping to make love to you," Linc reminded him. "I don't normally carry lube around in my pocket, though I may need to start."

Jonah frowned, and Linc kissed him. "Get undressed and let me see what I can find." He got up from the bed, and once again Jonah admired his backside as he walked toward the bathroom. Had it only been a day and a half since the last time?

He hurriedly stripped and tossed his clothes aside as Linc came out of the bathroom with a small bottle in hand. "Lube?" he asked eagerly.

"Hand lotion." He tossed the bottle to Jonah.

"Will that work?" Jonah asked uneasily.

"This isn't my first rodeo, darlin'. It won't work as well as Astroglide, but in a pinch, it'll serve. Now c'mere and get me prepped."

Jonah tried to remember what Linc had done for him, though Linc had to guide his fingers once he'd slicked them up. When Linc assured him he was ready, Jonah rolled the condom over his erection and knelt between Linc's knees.

Linc wedged a pillow beneath his back and then urged Jonah forward. "Just take it slow at first."

The sense of joining with Linc was more incredible than anything Jonah had ever felt. He pushed in as slowly as he could bear to, Linc's murmured words of praise coaxing him on. When he was fully sheathed, he leaned forward to kiss Linc deeply, as intimately connected as two people could possibly be. Linc pushed up against him, and after only a few thrusts, Jonah felt the pressure of his climax building. He tried to will it back, but it flooded through him, leaving him shaking against Linc's chest. When he caught his breath, he tried to pull away, but Linc held him in place, drawing their joined hands to his erection. It didn't take more than a few strokes for Linc to follow him in release.

"Shouldn't we have come together?" Jonah asked when he lay snuggled against Linc's chest after disposing of the condom and cleaning them up.

"Only if you want to make yourself crazy." Linc turned to press a kiss to Jonah's temple. "As long as we're both satisfied, what difference does it make who comes first?"

"I still think I should have been able to last longer."

"We'll have the rest of our lives for you to work on that," Linc reminded him.

Jonah twisted the ring Linc had placed on his finger. "The rest of our lives… that sounds like about enough time."

"Speaking of that," Linc said, his chest rumbling against Linc's ear, "we should start thinking about the kind of wedding you want."

"Couldn't we just elope?" Jonah suggested. The thought of enduring another big society event was enough to make his blood run cold, though he'd face it if that was what Linc expected.

"Have I told you how perfect you are?" Linc pushed up on an elbow for a kiss. "Eloise's description of the kind of circus she thinks is required for 'the proper Courtwright wedding' is enough to give me the shakes."

"Is she going to be a problem?"

Linc shrugged. "I reminded her yesterday that my father left the Broken Spoke to me, not to her, and she could accept that I would be asking you to marry me or find somewhere else to live. She may not be overjoyed, but I don't see her moving out anytime soon."

"I'd be happy to just get a license at the county courthouse," Jonah said. "I'd like to ask Wes and Sammy and Aidan to be there, but other than Caylee, that's all I need."

"Your parents?" Linc asked gently.

Jonah shook his head. "My mom's not ready to accept it. I hope she'll get there, eventually, but for now I think it's best to just let them know after the fact."

"We'll buy the license as soon as we get to Dallas tomorrow," Linc said. "I'd like Ford to be there as my best man, but I can call and tell him to meet us on Thursday."

"Thursday? Why not tomorrow?"

"Texas has a seventy-two-hour waiting period." Link sounded almost as disappointed as Jonah felt. "We could drive down to the ranch once we get the license, but unless you'd rather get married there, I'd just as soon let Eloise know after the fact too."

"It will be easier for Wes and Sammy and Aidan if we stay in Dallas."

Linc cradled Jonah's face in his palms and drew him into a long, slow kiss to seal the decision.

"At least we didn't lie to your parents," Linc said after he finally released Jonah's lips. "We do have some business to attend to that can't wait another day."

"I just hope Caylee won't mind staying at the townhouse until Thursday."

"If she isn't comfortable there, we'll get her a hotel room downtown, because you're not sleeping anywhere but at the condo with me."

Jonah couldn't think of anything that sounded more wonderful. "Should I set an alarm?"

Linc grinned. "You'd better. I plan to make love to you again before we shower in the morning—together this time. I'm not taking any chances on you running out on me again."

"I wouldn't dream of it," Jonah assured him.

"That's good, because I reckon there's still a thing or two I can teach you."

Epilogue

Eight months later

"HOW'S the little princess this afternoon?" Linc asked when Caylee came downstairs with Jolynn after her midday feeding.

"Ready for you to burp her." Caylee handed the infant off to Linc with a smile. "Do you have babysitting duty today?"

"Jonah will have to take over soon, and since Eloise isn't around to claim her, I thought I'd get my cuddles in now. I swear that woman couldn't love Jolynn any more if she were her own grandchild." Linc positioned the infant over his shoulder and patted her back gently. "That's a good girl!" he crooned when she belched loudly. "Ford and I are driving up to Lubbock this afternoon to look at some breeder bulls."

Jonah poked his head out from under the desk where he'd been trying to hook up the new computer he'd bought for their home office. "I think I've got it now. Let me be sure it boots up, and then I'll take her from you."

"Be sure everything is working first." Linc bounced Jolynn, making her coo with laughter. "You'll have the rest of the afternoon with her."

"I've got the second shift at the vet's office all week, one to six. Tell Wes he can't serve supper until I get back, or Ford will kill it all off again before I get any," Caylee complained.

"Do I hear someone disparaging my good name?" Ford entered the room through the kitchen doorway. "Hi, Caylee. Hey there, little sweet'ums. You're cuter than a sackful of puppies." He bent down to make googly faces at Jolynn, who burped again.

Linc chuckled. "So much for your way with women."

Ford ignored the teasing. "Where is Wes, anyway?" he asked. "I expected him to be here already."

"He went into town to get some ingredients he needed—" Jonah began when the front door opened and Wes came in, so loaded down with bags that only the top of his head, the hair dyed in ombré shades of green, was visible. "Speak of the devil...."

"Hey, purty little thing," Ford drawled, taking the groceries from Wes's arms and revealing a T-shirt that invited him to "French Kiss the Cook."

"Hey, tall, blond, and handsome. Put those on the counter for me, will you?" Wes ogled Ford's backside and winked at Jonah as he followed Ford into the kitchen.

Linc shook his head, and Jonah bent down and tickled Jolynn's bare feet. "I picked up the mail earlier, Cay. There's a package for you from Tarleton State."

"Good! It should be the information on class selection for the fall semester." She took the bulky envelope from Jonah and slipped it into her bag. "I'll look at it during my break."

"Eli will be glad to have someone help him with vaccinations come fall," Linc commented, handing Jolynn off to Jonah.

"He'll be glad to have an excuse to spend more time with Caylee," Jonah countered, laughing when Caylee's cheeks flushed.

"Don't you dare start matchmaking, Jonah Hollis-Courtwright," she warned him. "I'm swearing off men until I get my vet tech degree. Besides, if you and Linc decide you want a little one of your own, it'll be easier if I'm not involved with someone else."

"Let's enjoy this little one before we start thinking about surrogacy," Linc said. "Besides, you need time to take care of yourself. We're talking about another child, not a calving operation." He took Caylee's hands. "I don't ever want you to think you have to do this for us."

Caylee squeezed back. "Ask Jonah whether I've ever done anything I didn't want to do. When you decide you're ready, I'll be doing it because I love both of you."

Linc pulled Caylee into a hug, and she kissed his cheek. "I'd better get going. Tell Wes what I said about supper!"

"You be careful driving that beater." Jonah hugged Caylee before she headed out the door to work.

"So what is for supper?" Linc asked when Wes and Ford came out of the kitchen. If Wes's hair was even more tousled than usual, neither of them commented on it.

"Korean spare ribs with kalbi sauce, kimchi, and japchae."

Jonah hummed his approval, and Ford moaned. "You ready, boss? The sooner we leave, the sooner we'll get back and can start eating."

"I'll be with you directly." Linc took Jonah into his arms, careful not to jostle Jolynn, and gave him a slow kiss. "Don't work too hard while we're gone."

"Once Jolynn goes down for her nap, I'll get the printer hooked up and start going over the new lease returns for the second quarter. With the drop in oil and gas prices, I've been thinking we may want to consider diversifying into wind power too. The western ridge would be a perfect place to put some turbines."

"Letting you take on managing the energy holdings was the best decision I ever made." Linc kissed Jonah again. "After marrying you, of course."

"I can't argue with you there." Jonah swatted Linc on the rear. "Go buy us some bulls."

"As soon as Ford can drag himself away," Linc said dryly, watching the foreman release Wes from their own kiss.

"You and Jonah make domesticity look so good, I'm thinking of giving it a try myself," Ford said with a shrug. "Besides, you've tasted his cooking!"

"The way to a man's heart...," Wes said in a fair imitation of Ford's drawl.

Linc smiled. "I may have to start thinking about investing in a restaurant soon."

"Like the Y.O. Ranch!" Jonah said. "And Aidan can build it, and Sammy can design the graphics for the menus and the website."

"You two can plan it all out while we're gone." Linc was claiming a final kiss when Eloise's voice sounded from the hallway leading to the opposite end of the ranch house.

"Is Wesley here yet? I've found something fascinating!"

"What is it, Eloise?" Wes called back.

"Look here." She set her iPad onto the table and brought up an entry. "The *Linnet* sailed out of Plymouth to Boston in 1638. Look here at the passenger manifest. Arthur Edward Courtwright and family…."

"And Silas Paterson!" Wes crowed.

"What does that mean?" Ford sounded baffled.

"Our ancestors sailed to America together!" Eloise looked as delighted as Jonah had ever seen her.

"We're practically family!" Wes declared, giving her a hug.

Jonah had to smile. "I never thought I'd see the day," he told Linc happily.

"The best family is the one you choose yourself," Linc said. "And we chose pretty well, didn't we, darlin'?"

Coming in June 2016

꩜REAMSPUN DESIRES

#11

Finding Family by Connie Bailey

When you find your family, you'll do anything to keep it.

When Charles Macquarrie inherits a fortune and an international clothing company, he also inherits three young cousins he desperately needs help raising. By a stroke of luck, he discovers and hires Jonathan Lamb, who spent his life in a children's home due to chronic illness, to be his nanny.

If Jon thought a budding romance with his wealthy boss complicated his life, he has no idea of the hardships awaiting him when he's charged with embezzlement. But even when threatened by accounting discrepancies and mob connections, Jon and Charles won't let go of the family they've built together without a fight.

#12

Undercover Boyfriend by Jacob Z. Flores

Two men, one lie, and a whole bunch of trouble.

Marty Valdez is in serious trouble. His sister's wedding is around the corner, and everyone expects to meet Marty's super-successful underwear model boyfriend—who Marty invented. Now Marty has to produce a half-naked hottie or suffer the worst humiliation of his life.

FBI agent Luke Myers is in serious trouble. He's been working undercover to take down a dangerous drug cartel, but his cover's blown and he needs to disappear. Luckily, a geeky yet intriguing comic book artist gives him the perfect opportunity. Luke just has to pretend to be his boyfriend, and pretending is what he does best. But between Marty's mother and his ex, Luke might've bitten off more than he can chew, and Marty's knack for finding trouble might ruin more than just his sister's wedding.

www.dreamspinnerpress.com

Now Available

REAMSPUN DESIRES

#7

Forgive and Forget by Charlie Cochet

He's hot. He's dangerous. And he can't remember anything.

As the owner of Apple 'N Pies, Joe Applin leads a quiet, uneventful life, content to spend his days serving customers who come from all over to eat his delicious homemade pies. Along with his motley crew—Bea, Elsie, and Donnie—Joe couldn't be happier in his little kingdom of baked goods and java.

Experience has taught Joe that love is overrated—and at times dangerous. He has no intention of repeating past mistakes. But then he meets the mysterious, handsome man with no name and no memories, and Joe can't deny something sweet is in the works. He isn't one to take risks, not with his heart and certainly not with his life, but the more time he spends with "Tom," the closer he is to losing both.

#8

Unstable Stud by Ariel Tachna

Horses were his passion, until he laid eyes on his boss.

Eighteen months ago, tragedy struck Bywater Farm when a riding accident killed Clay Hunter's lover and traumatized his prize horse, King of Hearts. Clay and King lingered in limbo, surviving but not really living, until a breath of fresh air in the form of Luke Davis, a new groom in the stud barn, revives them both.

When a fall from King's back sends Luke to the emergency room, Clay watches the shaky foundation of their budding relationship tumble down. Can Clay really love a jockey again, or will his fear of losing another man he loves keep them apart for good?

www.dreamspinnerpress.com

Love Always Finds a Way

(DREAMSPUN DESIRES
Subscription Service

Love eBooks?

Our monthly subscription service
gives you two eBooks per month for
one low price. Each month's titles
will be automatically delivered
to your Dreamspinner Bookshelf
on their release dates.

Prefer print?

Receive two paperbacks per month!
Both books ship on the 1st of the
month, giving you *exclusive* early
access! As a bonus, you'll receive
both eBooks on their release dates!

Visit
www.dreamspinnerpress.com
for more info or to sign up now!

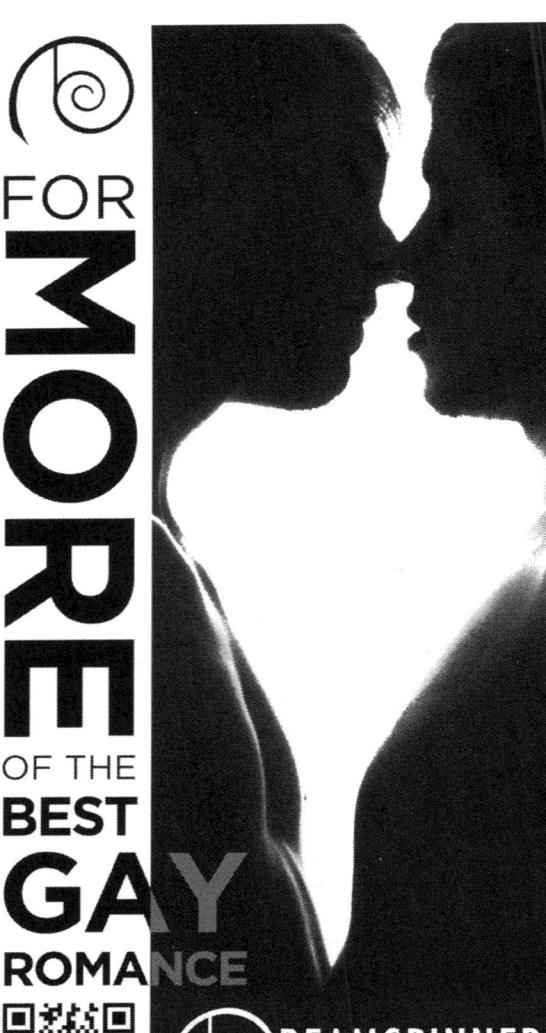

Made in United States
Orlando, FL
22 March 2026

79559142R00127